"You can't expect me to give up six months of my life for you!"

Andreas gazed at Carrie pityingly. "You should have thought of that before you began your vendetta against me. I am a good man. I am loyal to my family and my friends. I do not cheat in life or in love. But I am not a man to cross and you, *matia mou*, have crossed me and now you must accept the consequences."

She shook her head blankly before looking at him. "You can't want to marry me."

"I have no wish to marry at all, least of all to a poisonous viper like you."

"Then *don't.*"

"I will do whatever is necessary to protect my business and my reputation." He rolled his shoulders and looked at her. "I've been waiting more than fifteen years for the freedom to do whatever the hell I want. I can wait another six months for it. And, you know, I think a marriage to you could be fun."

Michelle Smart's love affair with books started when she was a baby, when she would cuddle them in her cot. A voracious reader of all genres, she found her love of romance established when she stumbled across her first Harlequin book at the age of twelve. She's been reading—and writing—them ever since. Michelle lives in Northamptonshire, England, with her husband and two young Smarties.

Books by Michelle Smart

Harlequin Presents

Once a Moretti Wife

Bound to a Billionaire

Protecting His Defiant Innocent
Claiming His One-Night Baby
Buying His Bride of Convenience

Brides for Billionaires

Married for the Greek's Convenience

One Night With Consequences

Claiming His Christmas Consequence

Wedlocked!

Wedded, Bedded, Betrayed

The Kalliakis Crown

Talos Claims His Virgin
Theseus Discovers His Heir
Helios Crowns His Mistress

Visit the Author Profile page
at Harlequin.com for more titles.

Michelle Smart

—

A BRIDE AT HIS BIDDING

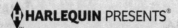

HARLEQUIN PRESENTS®

Recycling programs
for this product may
not exist in your area.

ISBN-13: 978-1-335-50407-4

A Bride at His Bidding

First North American Publication 2018

Copyright © 2018 by Michelle Smart

Printed in U.S.A.

www.Harlequin.com

A BRIDE AT HIS BIDDING

CHAPTER ONE

ANDREAS SAMARAS POKED his head into the adjoining office to his own. Having spent the day on a multinational conference call, he needed to check in with his PA.

'How is everything going?'

Debbie sighed. 'The world is going to hell in a handcart.'

'Quite.' His PA's theatrical tendencies were infamous throughout Samaras Fund Management. Andreas would find it wearing if she weren't the best business PA he'd ever had. 'Apart from that, is there anything I need to know? With regards to the business,' he hastened to add in case she started harping on about polar bears and Arctic ice melt again.

'Nothing important.'

'Good. How did the interviews go? Have you come up with a shortlist for me?' Rochelle, his domestic PA, had quit. The smitten fool was getting married and had decided that a job requiring a great deal of travel was not a good fit for domestic bliss. He'd offered to double her wages and increase her holidays but still she had said no. He'd dragged his heels for weeks about finding a replacement for her in the hope she would change her mind. She hadn't and finally he had accepted defeat.

Debbie held up a stack of papers. 'I've whittled the candidates down to five.'

Andreas stepped into the office. Debbie had been tasked with doing the preliminary interviews. She knew exactly what kind of person he was looking for to take on the role that basically entailed organising his domestic life. It was a live-in role that would see the successful candidate travel wherever he went, ensuring his domestic life ran as smoothly as his business. The person needed to be honest, loyal, unobtrusive and flexible, have impeccable references, a clean driving licence and no criminal record.

He took the papers from her hand and flipped through them. All had a square photograph of the candidate attached to the corner of their applications. It was a requirement he insisted on. Three candidates would make it to the shortlist and he liked to be familiar with their appearance before he met them for the final interview, which he would undertake personally.

By Debbie's computer was a stack of the applicants she'd already rejected. The top one caught his eye. There was something familiar about the direct gaze staring back...

'Why have you rejected this one?' he asked, picking up the form and studying it. Dark hazel eyes stared right back at him. Dark hazel eyes he knew instinctively that he'd seen before.

Debbie peered at it with a frown. 'Oh, her. Caroline Dunwoody. She interviewed well but there was something about her I didn't trust. I don't know what it was. A feeling, nothing more, but it made me check her references in more detail. One of them checks out okay but I'm suspicious of the other one. She says she worked as Head of Housekeeping at Hargate Manor for two years and has a letter in her file to that effect. I spoke to the gentleman who wrote the reference, the Manor's butler, and he verified everything.'

'Then what's the problem?'

'Hargate Manor doesn't exist.'

His eyebrows rose. 'Doesn't exist?'

'There is no Hargate Manor within fifty miles of this one's supposed location.'

If Debbie said it didn't exist then it didn't exist. She was the most thorough person Andreas knew.

He looked more closely at Caroline Dunwoody's photograph, racking his brain trying to remember where he could have met her. He usually had an excellent recall for faces but on this occasion he couldn't put a finger on it. She had dark chestnut hair that fell in a neat line to her shoulders and pretty if angular features, a short straight nose, a top lip slightly fuller than the bottom and a cute heart-shaped chin. Yes, a pretty face but not one familiar to him.

But he had seen those eyes before.

Just as he opened his mouth to order Debbie to do some more digging into this woman, it suddenly came to him.

Digging. Journalists did lots of digging.

Caroline. The extended version of Carrie.

Carrie Rivers. The journalist sister of his niece's old best friend.

The journalist for the *Daily Times* who had made a name for herself by exposing the illegal and often seedy practices of rich businessmen.

He doubted he would still remember their tenuous association were it not that her most recent undercover investigation into James Thomas, an old business acquaintance of his, had revealed James's business to be a cover for drugs, arms and people trafficking. A month ago, Carrie's meticulous work had seen James sentenced to fifteen years in prison. Andreas had read about the sentencing and silently cheered. He hoped he rotted in his cell.

With the feeling of a ball bearing pressing down on his guts, Andreas did an Internet search on his phone for her. There were no photographs of Carrie online. He supposed this wasn't surprising given the nature of her work.

But it was her. He was certain of it.

He'd only met Carrie once, three years ago. It had been such a fleeting moment that it was no surprise he'd struggled to remember. Three years ago, she had been blonde with rounded cheeks.

Her eyes were the only thing about her that hadn't changed. Their gazes had met as he'd left the headmistress's office of his niece's boarding school. Carrie and her sister Violet had been sat in the corridor waiting for their turn to be admitted. Violet had hung her head in shame when she'd seen him. Carrie should have hung her head too.

Neither had known it would be the last time they would be admitted into the headmistress's office. Violet was to be expelled with immediate effect.

Three years on and Carrie was applying for a domestic job with him under a different name and supplying fake references in the process. This did not bode well and his brain groped for reasons as to why she might now be targeting him. Andreas ran a clean business. He paid all his taxes, both personal and corporation, in all the relevant jurisdictions. He followed and exceeded local employment law. His romantic affairs over the years had been consensual and discreet, guilt and responsibility for his family overriding the urge to bed as many beautiful women as possible, something he intended to rectify now all the burdens had been lifted from his shoulders.

One thing Andreas had learned over his thirty-seven years was that when problems cropped up, the only thing to do was keep a clear head and deal with them immediately, stopping the problems escalating into catastrophe.

A plan quickly formed in his mind. He inhaled deeply then smiled. 'Debbie, I want you to call Miss Dunwoody and invite her back for a second interview.'

Debbie looked at him as if he'd sprouted blossom from his head.

'Back it up with a letter. This is what I want you to say...'

Carrie sat in the spacious reception room of Samaras Fund Management's London headquarters and tried to get air into lungs that seemed to have forgotten how to breathe. Her heart was beating erratically, the thuds loud in her ears, and she had to keep wiping her clammy palms on her thighs.

She'd woken from fractured sleep with her stomach churning so hard she'd had to force her coffee down. Food had been unthinkable.

She had never known nerves like it, although calling this sensation nerves was like calling a river a small trickle of water. Soon she would be taken through to Andreas Samaras's office and she had to contain these mixed and virulent emotions that threatened to crush her.

She hadn't suffered any nerves while going undercover and investigating James Thomas. She'd been ice-cool and focussed as she'd systematically gathered the evidence needed to prove his heinous crimes and expose him, using the same mind-set she used on her regular investigations, her focus never swaying. The day James had been sentenced had been the brightest spot of the last three nightmarish years.

Andreas might not have fed her sister the drugs that had destroyed her young fragile body but his contribution to Violet's descent into hell had been every bit as lethal as James's and far more personal, and now it was his turn for justice. Carrie could not allow her nerves or conscience to blow it for her…but this time it was different.

It had been common knowledge that James Thomas was a shady figure deserving of proper investigation. Getting permission and backing to go undercover in his workforce had been easy—the whole of the *Daily Times* had wanted that scumbag brought down.

Andreas Samaras, Greek billionaire investor and owner of Samaras Fund Management, was a different kettle of fish. There was nothing in his past or on the rumour mill to suggest he was anything other than clean. Only Carrie knew differently, and when she'd seen the advertisement for a Domestic PA mere days after James had been sentenced, she had known Andreas's time had come. She knew infiltrating his personal life carried a much greater risk than investigating him as an employee in his business life but it was a risk she was willing to take.

Three years ago she had written two names on a piece of paper. She had since struck James's name off. Now it was time to strike Andreas's off too.

To get her newspaper's backing to go undercover though, she'd had to tell a little white lie… A few surprised eyebrows had been raised but the go-ahead had been given. No one had disbelieved her.

As the clock ticked down to the moment she would be taken to see Andreas, the ramifications of her lie rang loudly in her head. If the truth that Carrie was undertaking a personal vendetta was revealed her career would be over.

The *Daily Times* was no shady tabloid. It was a highbrow publication that had made it through the trials and tribulations all the British press had been through over the past decade with its reputation largely intact. It was a good employer too.

If they could print only a fraction of what was suspected about some of the world's most powerful people the public would need vodka spiked into the water system to help them get over the shock. The rich and powerful threw money into silencing the press and making problems disappear. They forced their staff to sign cast-iron non-disclosure agreements and were ruthless about enforcing them. Super-injunctions were *de rigueur.*

If Carrie got the job with Andreas she would be thrown directly into his personal world. She would be closer to her target than on any of her prior investigations. Who knew what she would find? When she'd first gone undercover with James in his accounts department she'd known he was a drug-abuser with a predilection for teenage girls but had had no idea of his involvement with people trafficking or arms. Andreas was that criminal's friend. Who knew what *he* was involved with?

She'd known the odds of getting the job with Andreas were slim, even with her rigged CV and falsified references. On paper, they'd made her the perfect candidate for the role but it had been a rushed job, hurried to meet the application deadline. She couldn't help worrying that there was a giant hole or two in it.

She hadn't thought the preliminary interview with his PA had gone well and had left the building certain she'd messed up. When she'd received the call inviting her to a second interview, she was so shocked a mere breeze would have knocked her over.

And now, as that ticking clock echoed louder in her ears, all she could see when she closed her eyes was the burning hatred Andreas had thrown her way the one time their eyes had met.

'Miss Dunwoody?'

Carrie blinked and looked up to find the superior young receptionist staring at her quizzically.

She'd gone under the name of Rivers for so long it had become a part of herself. Hearing her real name sounded foreign. She'd been known by the surname of Rivers since her mother had remarried when she'd been four and had thought it wise to continue using it when she embarked on her career in investigative journalism. There were a lot of sickos out there. In this instance, that decision had been fortuitous. She'd never legally changed her name. People in her world knew her as Carrie Rivers. Her birth certificate, driving licence and passport had her as Caroline Dunwoody. The advert for the job had explicitly stated it involved lots of travelling.

Falsifying references was one thing. Trying to fake a passport was a whole different ballpark.

'Mr Samaras is ready to see you now.'

He'd kept her waiting for an hour.

Swallowing back a sudden violent burst of nausea, Carrie tightly clutched the strap of her handbag and followed the receptionist down a wide corridor lined with modern artwork.

It had taken her ages to find the perfect outfit for this interview. She'd wanted to look professional but not as if she were applying for a job within Samaras Fund Management itself. She'd settled on a cream high-necked cashmere top with a dozen small buttons running the length, a pair of smart grey trousers and simple black heels that gave her a little extra height for confidence but which she could comfortably walk in. Now she felt as if she'd dressed in a smothering straightjacket, the heels a hindrance to her unsteady feet.

A door opened and Carrie was admitted into an office twice the size of the one she shared with the rest of the crime team and a hundred times plusher.

There, behind an enormous oak desk, working on one of three computers, sat Andreas Samaras.

Her heart slammed against her chest then thudded painfully and for one frightening moment Carrie thought she really was going to vomit.

He didn't look up from what he was doing.

'One minute please,' he said in the deep, quick, sharply staccato voice she remembered from their one telephone conversation instigated by Andreas five years ago.

Carrie's sister and Andreas's niece had been weekly boarders and roommates at school together. Their friendship had deepened and soon they had wanted to spend weekends and holidays together too. Andreas had phoned Carrie to agree on some ground rules. They had found much to agree on. It helped that they had both been in the same position, both of them the sole carers of their vulnerable teenage charges. After that one conversation, they would text message each other to confirm if Natalia was due at Carrie's for the weekend or if Violet was due at Andreas's. It had become a rhythm in Carrie's life, right until Andreas had engineered Violet's expulsion.

Finally, he looked up from his computer, pushed his chair back and got to his feet. The sheer size and power of the man was as starkly apparent as it had been when he had swept past her three years ago.

'It is a pleasure to meet you, Miss Dunwoody.'

She stared at the huge hand extending towards her and forced herself to lean forward and take it. Large, warm tapered fingers covered hers as he shook her hand briskly before letting go.

'Take a seat,' he commanded amicably, sitting back down and picking up a thin pile of papers from his desk.

The skin on her hand buzzed where he'd clasped it and she fought the urge to rub it against her thigh as she took the seat he'd directed her to, and expelled the tiniest sigh of relief.

There had been only a teeny ounce of doubt he wouldn't recognise her. Physically she'd changed a lot since that one fleeting glance three years ago outside the headmistress's office, when his light brown eyes had lasered her with such ferocity she had recoiled. Stress alone had made her lose three stone since then, which had altered her facial features as well as her body shape. She'd long stopped her quest for the perfect shade of blonde hair and reverted to her natural brown colour.

If Andreas had the slightest idea of who she

really was, she would not be there. She wouldn't
have got past the initial application.

It hadn't seemed feasible that he would recognise her or her name but she had learned
through five years of her job to take nothing
for granted.

Light brown thoughtful eyes studied her
rather than the paperwork in his hand, which
she guessed was a copy of her job application,
and she fought hard against the flush of colour crawling over her skin. When she finally
forced herself to meet his gaze, the raw masculinity staring back at her intensified the flush,
enflaming her bones, taking her so unawares
that for a moment her mind emptied of everything but the rapid tattoo of her heart reverber-
ating in her ears.

Carrie swallowed, desperate for moisture in
her parched throat, desperate to suck air into
lungs that had closed in on themselves. Whatever kind of a man Andreas was, there was no
denying that he was divine to look at. He had
thick dark brown hair sun-kissed on the tips,
barely tamed to flop onto a gently lined forehead, cheekbones you could ski down, a chis-
elled square jaw already dark with stubble and
a sharp nose with a slight bend on the bridge.
Deeply tanned and weather-beaten, he looked
every one of his thirty-seven years.

He was the most overtly virile and handsome man she'd ever laid eyes on.

Then he gave her a crooked grin.

It was like being smiled at by the big bad wolf the moment before he ate Grandma.

'Congratulations on making it to the final shortlist,' he said in his impeccable English. Carrie knew, as she knew so much about this man, that he'd learned English at school in his Greek homeland and then perfected it at his American university. He spoke the language with true fluency, firing the words out so quickly his accent sounded like a musical cadence to her ears. 'I will be honest and tell you that you are my preferred candidate.'

She was taken aback. 'I am?'

His eyes sparkled. 'Before I go into more detail about my requirements, there are things I wish to know about you.'

She attempted to hide her fear with a smile that didn't want to form on her frozen cheeks.

Had he spotted the holes in her résumé?

After a moment of silence that seemed to echo between them she got her paper-dry throat to work. 'What do you want to know?'

'References and application forms only give a narrow perspective on a person. If I give you the job then we will spend a lot of time together. You will be my right hand in my domestic life.

You will be privy to my most intimate secrets. So, Miss Dunwoody…may I call you Caroline?'

She nodded faintly. The only person who had ever called her Caroline had been her mother but she hadn't made her name sing as Andreas did. Even as it occurred to her, that struck Carrie as an odd thought to have.

'Caroline. If I give you the job I need to trust you and trust that we'll be able to work well together.' His relaxed frame, the musical staccato of his voice and the amusement enlivening his handsome features all worked together to reassure her that her ruse had worked but the scent of danger still lingered.

Her instincts were telling her to take her bag and coat and leave this office right now.

'Are you married or do you have a partner?' he continued. 'I ask because if you do, you should know you will be spending a lot of time apart from them. Your personal life must be conducted in your own time and you won't have much of that.'

'I have no significant other.' She never had and never would. Men could not be trusted. She'd learned that before she'd reached double digits.

'Children?'

She shook her head, immediately thinking of

Violet, who she loved as much as if she'd given birth to her.

'Any other dependants? Dogs, cats, goldfish?'

'No.'

'Good. I make no apologies. I am a demanding employer and this job is a twenty-four-seven one. What did Debbie tell you about it in the preliminary interview?'

'That it entails the day-to-day running of your homes.'

His head tilted and his face grew thoughtful. 'That is how the job is advertised but you should know it is more about the day-to-day running of *me*. My domestic PA does oversee the running of my homes but they're not expected to do any of the manual chores themselves—I employ other domestic staff for that. I work long and demanding hours. When I am at home I like to live in comfort and I want all my needs and comforts met by someone who is capable of turning their hand to anything, without argument. I need someone on hand to tend to all my personal needs—pour my drinks, prepare my clothing for me, make sure a towel is on hand if I do any physical activity, that kind of thing.'

It wasn't a domestic PA the man wanted, Carrie thought in mute outrage as she listened to his seductive voice, it was a slave.

'In return, I offer a *very* generous salary.' He

mentioned a figure that made her blink, it being four times what she earned at the newspaper.

She imagined that any genuine applicant would bite his hand off for it. It was an extortionate amount of money for what was essentially nothing more than being Andreas's dogsbody.

Now he put a forearm on his desk and leaned forward to stare at her with an intensity that made her stomach do a strange flip.

The more she looked into his eyes, the more startling she found them, the light brown having a translucent quality that still contained real depth.

If he gave her the job she would have to tread carefully for as long as she lived under his roof. This man was dangerous.

'Now, Caroline,' he said, the tempo of his speech finally slowing down a notch, 'I do have one more requirement from the person I give this role to.'

'Which is?'

'I require someone who has a cheerful disposition.'

She might as well leave, then. How could she be cheerful around the man who'd caused such damage?

'What I mean by that is that I get enough stress in my work life. When I come home I like to be welcomed with a smile and not be bothered by petty gripes. *Can* you smile?'

He framed the question with such faux earnestness that Carrie found her facial muscles softening and the smile she'd been trying to produce since she'd stepped into his office breaking out of its own accord.

His eyes gleamed in response. 'Much better.' Then he sat back and folded his arms across his chest. The cuffs of his sleeves moved with the motion revealing a tantalising glimpse of fine dark hair.

He nodded slowly. 'Yes. I think you're going to suit me very well. The job is yours if you want it.'

She blinked her gaze away from his arms as his words sank in. 'It is?'

She hadn't expected it to be this easy...

Her heart started to thunder beneath her ribs. This was *too* easy.

Andreas was one of the richest men in the world. He was highly intelligent—unverified reports placed his IQ in the world's top one per cent and he had the street smarts to match it. In short, he was no fool, and this job that he was giving her after less than fifteen minutes in his company would take her straight into the heart of his life.

'*Do* you want it?' he challenged, breaking the silence that had fallen.

'Yes.' She nodded for emphasis, trying to muster her enthusiasm, and forced another smile to her face. 'Yes, I do, definitely. Thank you.'

'Good.' His teeth flashed wolfishly. 'Did you bring your passport?'

'Yes.' The letter discussing the second interview had been specific about it. She assumed it was needed for him to photocopy as proof of her identity.

Andreas rose to his feet. 'Then let us go. We have a flight slot to fill.'

Carrie stared at him blankly. 'Go?'

'The letter you were sent clearly explained that the successful candidate for the job would start immediately.'

'It did…' But she hadn't thought immediately meant *this* immediately. 'Are we going abroad *now*?'

That gleam she was beginning to seriously distrust flashed in his eyes again. 'Yes. Right now. Do you have a problem with that?'

'No problem.' She hurried to stand. The job was hers and she wouldn't give him reason to change his mind. She would practise smiling as soon as she found a mirror. 'It's just that I have no change of clothes with me.'

'You will be provided with everything you

need when we get there. Give Debbie your dress size as we leave.'

'Where are we going?'

'To one of my homes where it isn't raining.' And with that he opened his office door and ushered her through it.

door, 'when we get there. Give Debbie until five
time is we leave.'

'Where are we going?'

In one of my homes, where it isn't amusing.
And with that he opened his office door and
ushered her to

CHAPTER TWO

ANDREAS SAT AT his desk on his private jet with
his laptop open before him. Barely ten feet
away, Carrie was at the dining table reading
through the thick folder that contained the working details of all his properties. He had no doubt
she would find it excruciatingly tedious to read
through.

All his properties were listed except one—
the one they were flying to.

'Which one should I concentrate on?' she'd
asked when he'd given it to her, subtly letting
him know he hadn't given her their final des-
tination.

'All of them.' He'd smiled. 'I'll give you a test
when we arrive.'

'Which will be when?'

He'd looked at his watch. 'In approximately
eleven hours.'

Her eyes had flickered but she'd made no further comment. He'd seen her thoughts racing

and had enjoyed watching her bite the questions back.

He'd enjoyed himself enormously throughout their meeting too, far more than he'd expected. The knowledge that he'd rumbled her before she'd even set foot in his office had bubbled away inside him, satisfying enough to smother the anger that had fought for an outlet.

Anger clouded logical thinking and he needed to keep his mind clear if he was to continue outwitting this viper.

He'd determined that getting her out of England and as far from her home and true employment as he could and as quickly as he could was the best way to proceed. Disorientate her. Put her at the disadvantage without her even realising it and then, when he had her in his private home, unable to escape or communicate with the outside world, he would demand answers. He wanted to know everything—why she was investigating him, what she expected to find and who had put her up to it. He'd made his own discreet enquiries amongst his media contacts but had come up blank. No one was aware of even a hint of a brewing scandal about him.

Instinct told him that Carrie's reasons for being here were at least partly personal. The coincidence was too great to be explained any other way.

He would discover her reasons in due course but rather than question her immediately, he decided he'd have some fun with her first. Let her suffer a little. It was the least she deserved.

Did Carrie really think him such a useless human being that he required someone to live by his side pouring his drinks and mopping his brow? Andreas liked his creature comforts but he was no man-child and he'd seen the flicker of surprise in her eyes when he'd outlined the duties expected of her, duties he'd made up on the spur of the moment just to see what her reaction would be.

For the next few days he would embrace the man-child role and make her wait on him hand and foot. She would hate every minute of it.

Excellent.

He would enjoy every minute of it.

He watched her put aside the notepad she'd been scribbling on as she'd read through the folder and remove her phone from her handbag. She angled her body away from him and switched it on. A few moments later her shoulders rose and she tugged at her hair.

Andreas grinned, enjoying her silent frustration to find it not working. He dealt with highly sensitive information. To get onto his jet's network required a password. He wondered how long it would be before she cracked and asked for it.

It took her three hours, an impressive length of time he thought, before she lifted her head, cleared her throat, and said, 'Would it be possible for me to have the Wi-Fi password?'

'I didn't think you had anybody to check in with,' he commented idly, enjoying the flush of colour that crawled up her slender neck.

'I don't,' she said with only the smallest of hesitation. 'I just wanted to check my emails.'

'Expecting anything important?'

She shook her head, her whole neck now aflame. 'Don't worry about it. I'll check them later.'

Carrie Rivers, Caroline Dunwoody, whatever her real name was, had a beautiful neck. He'd seen by her photograph that she was pretty but in the flesh she was so much more, her features softer, her skin dewy and golden. She was beautiful.

He thought back to the slightly plump woman he'd caught that momentary glimpse of three years back. Her eyes had been striking enough for him to remember but at the time he'd been too angry to think properly let alone remember any other detail about her. He'd been angrier than he'd ever been. The previous evening, he'd come home early from a rare evening out to find his niece and her best friend off their heads on drink and drugs. What had followed later that night had been almost as bad.

Taking guardianship of an orphaned teenage girl had never been easy but that weekend had been the hardest of his life, harder even than the night he'd received the call telling him his sister and brother-in-law had been found dead or the day he'd learned his parents faced financial ruin.

Where was the manual that gave step-by-step guidance on how to handle the discovery that your niece, your responsibility, was creeping towards drug addiction, or how to handle waking to find your niece's sixteen-year-old best friend naked in your bedroom intent on seducing you? Where had Violet learned that kind of behaviour? From her older sister? Was the seemingly prim and proper woman sitting just feet away from him as wanton and reckless as her sister had been?

Despite his best attempts, he'd been unable to discover anything significant about Carrie. Her page on the *Daily Times* website listed her awards and achievements but nothing of a personal nature. He only knew her age because of their old personal links. Twenty-six. An incredibly young age to have achieved so much in her career. That took real commitment and dedication, something he would have admired had those traits not now been aimed at him. But unlike the men—and they had *all* been men—she'd brought down before him, Andreas had nothing to hide. His business was clean. So why had she set her sights on him? Why was the award-winning investigative journalist Carrie Rivers after him? *Was* this personal?

Whatever the reasons, he would learn them and nip whatever trouble was brewing in the bud. The old maxim of keep your friends close but your enemies closer stood the test of time.

Until he learned the truth, he would keep Carrie *very* close to him and then…

And then, unless he could think of a better plan than the one formulating in his head, Carrie would be kept close by his side for the foreseeable future.

It was dark when they landed. The early spring storms London had been dealing with were but a distant memory as Carrie disembarked Andreas's jet and found herself engulfed in a heat the like of which she had only ever read about. She removed her jacket and looked up to find a cloudless black sky glittering with stars.

'Where are we?' She'd diligently read the folder Andreas had given her, pored over the location of all his homes and, as time had extended on their flight, convinced herself they were going to Tokyo.

'The Seychelles.' Andreas stood beside her. 'Welcome to Mahe, the largest island of the Seychelles Granitic Archipelago.'

Her mind turned frantically. How could she have missed a home in the Seychelles? She'd read his property folder from cover to cover three times, and there had been nothing about a home there in any of her prior investigations into him.

'It's the most private of my properties,' he said in a low voice close to her ear. The tangy freshness of his expensive cologne swirled around her.

Carrie casually sidestepped away from him and swallowed the sudden rush of moisture filling her mouth. 'What time is it?'

'One in the morning. We have a short flight on my helicopter before we reach my home.'

They were whisked through security and within twenty minutes of landing were climbing into a sparkling helicopter.

'Have you been in a helicopter before?' Andreas asked as he strapped himself in beside her.

There were six seats to choose from and he had to sit right next to her?

Carrie shook her head and determinedly did

not look at the thigh resting so close to her own she could feel its warmth on her skin.

'It's an enjoyable experience and the quickest way to my island.'

'*Your* island?'

He pulled a thoughtful face. 'It's more of a peninsular off another island but the peninsular belongs in its entirety to me.'

Carrie silently swore as, under the heavy noise of the rotors twirling, the helicopter lifted off the ground.

She hadn't had an inkling about any of this. What else had she missed in her research on him?

Whose name had this property and accompanying land been bought in? Was it a secret shell company? She would get digging into it as soon as she had some privacy and a decent Internet signal. She needed to check in with her editor and let him know where she was too. But after she'd had a shower and, hopefully, some sleep. She'd been in the same clothes for almost a whole day, not having dreamt when she dressed that morning that she would end the day in the famed wedding and honeymoon spot of the Seychelles.

By contrast, Andreas had showered an hour before landing and changed from his suit into a fresh, crisp white shirt and light grey tailored trousers.

She dragged her attention away from the powerful body brushing so close against her own and the tangy scent playing under her nose by envisaging the shower she would have when they reached his home. She wouldn't have the temperature scalding as she usually did. To rid herself of the stickiness clinging to her pores she would lather herself under refreshingly cool water.

Her thoughts dissolved as a particularly sharp movement from the pilot caused Andreas's thigh and arm to compact against hers. An immediate shock of awareness crashed through her, so acute and so sudden and so totally unexpected that she froze.

It felt as if she'd been tasered.

For long moments she couldn't breathe.

A large hand covered hers and squeezed.

'It's nothing to worry about,' he murmured. 'Just a little turbulence.'

Carrie swallowed and forced a nod, trying desperately to get a coherent thought into her scrambled brain, her lungs finally opening back up again when he let go of her hand.

She was just tired, she assured herself, digging her nails into her palms.

Better he think she'd been frightened by the sudden turbulence they'd flown into than know of the turbulence that had exploded inside her at the feel of him pressed so tightly against her.

She looked out of the window and made an effort to relax her frame.

Come on, Carrie. You've always wanted to fly in a helicopter. At least try *and enjoy it.*

Violet had always wanted to fly in a helicopter too. She remembered how excited her sister would get during sunny days when their mother was still alive and they would go out for walks and spot helicopters zooming overhead. Her chubby little arms would wave frantically and she was always convinced the pilots waved back.

What was Violet doing at that moment? Her sister had been in California for three months now, her recovery from addiction and all her other issues a slow, fragile process. Carrie had called her a couple of days ago, their weekly conversation as stilted and awkward as they had been since Violet had woken from her coma and it was spelled out how close to death she had come. Whenever she spoke to her sister now it was like talking to a stranger. The little girl whose first word had been 'Cawwie,' and who had followed Carrie like a shadow from the moment she could crawl was gone. In truth, she'd been gone for a long time and it tore at Carrie's heart to remember the sweetness that had once been there.

Blinking away hot tears at all that had been lost, Carrie continued to gaze out of the window. The moon was bright, allowing her to see the small landmass they were approaching in the middle of the Indian Ocean. Soon they flew directly over a beach gleaming white under the moonlight, the form of a large house emerging from the shadows as the pilot brought the helicopter down.

Andreas got out first then held out his hand to assist her, his eyes holding hers with a look that made her stomach knot in on itself.

Knowing she didn't have any choice, she took the hand. His fingers tightened as they wrapped around hers, solid and warm, keeping her steady as her feet reached for the ground.

'Thank you,' she muttered, glad the darkness cloaked her flaming cheeks from his probing gaze.

'My pleasure.' His fingertips swept gently over hers as he released his hold and then he climbed back inside to speak to his pilot.

Alone for a moment, Carrie inhaled deeply and found her senses filled with the heady scent of unseen flowers. The breeze of the ocean had cleared the humidity away, a fresh warmth brushing over her skin. It was all she could do not to close her eyes and savour the feeling.

Savouring the feeling would have to wait as

suddenly lights came on and Andreas's house—villa—mansion—which the pilot had landed in the back garden of, was revealed.

It was breathtaking.

Only two storeys high, what it lacked in height it made up for in width, looking like a white stonewashed Buddhist temple surrounded by a deep red wraparound veranda. Matching deep red roof tiles gave what could easily have been an imposing building a welcoming air.

Andreas had rejoined her. She could feel his eyes on her and knew he was looking for a reaction.

What kind of reaction would a true employee give?

She opted for a truthful one.

'It's lovely.'

'Isn't it?' he agreed. 'Wait until you see it in the daylight. I fell in love with it from a photograph. I was looking for a holiday home and here I've found the perfect place. I can get away from the world but there's people and nightlife only a short flight or boat ride away.'

'This is your holiday home?'

'Of course,' he said with mild surprise. 'Who would want to conduct business on a paradise like this?'

'How long will we be here?'

'Why? Is there somewhere you have to be?'

'No, it's just…' She felt herself getting flustered.

'Relax. I'm teasing you. I know you have no commitment you have to rush back for or you would have disclosed it on your application form. We'll stay here for a while. I haven't had a proper holiday in some time and need to recharge my batteries.'

She hadn't had a holiday in some time either. At least a decade, two or three years before her mother had died.

But this wasn't a holiday for her. She was here to work. Her job was to ensure the smooth running of this beautiful mansion and take care of the whims of its owner while secretly undertaking her own work of discovering its owner's darkest secrets. What kind of secrets she would find in Andreas's holiday home was anyone's guess. Chances were she would have to wait until they moved on to one of his other homes where he actually conducted business before she discovered anything useful.

Expecting a member of his staff to greet them—all his homes had at least three permanent live-in employees—Carrie was a little disconcerted to step inside and find the house shrouded in silence. Yes, it was the middle of the night, but surely the staff wouldn't retire for the night before their boss's arrival?

'I'll give you a quick tour before I show you

to our bedrooms,' Andreas said, leading the way. He headed through an arched doorway without a door and said, 'Here's the living area.'

Her misgivings were put to one side as she slowly took in the beauty of Andreas's house, a home that managed to be both luxurious and yet welcoming. High ceilings and white walls were given colour by an intricate tiled mosaic that covered the floor wherever they stepped, including the large, airy dining room dominated by a large, highly polished mahogany table.

The kitchen was the size of an entire floor of her home.

'This is Brendan's domain,' he informed her.

'Brendan's your chef?'

'Yes. If you're hungry I can call him and he'll make something for you.'

'I'm fine, thank you.' Regular meals, which she'd had to force down into her cramped stomach, had been provided throughout the flight by Andreas's cabin crew.

He shrugged. 'If you need anything before morning I'm sure you won't have any trouble finding it. I assume the kitchen functions as a normal kitchen.'

'You assume?'

He pulled a face. 'I employ staff so I don't have to do these chores for myself.'

'When was the last time you used a kitchen?'

she asked before she could stop herself. Somehow, she doubted Andreas welcomed his domestic employees questioning him.

Her doubt proved wrong.

'In my university days in America—I studied at MIT—I discovered I was a terrible cook so I got a job working as a waiter in an Italian restaurant where they were always happy to feed me. I've not cooked for myself since.'

'An *Italian* restaurant?'

'There were no decent Greek restaurants where I lived then. There was a tapas bar but they didn't do breakfast so I opted for the Italian one.'

His long legs powered on gracefully up the cantilevered stairs to the first floor. Carrie hurried behind him, smothering a yawn. All the travelling on top of minimal sleep had exhausted her.

'My room.' Andreas pushed open a door to reveal a bedroom equal in size to the kitchen, containing everything a spoiled billionaire could need. Carrie hung back, reluctant to enter until he beckoned her inside with the crook of his finger and the hint of a gleam in his piercing light brown eyes. 'Don't be shy, Caroline. You need to become familiar with my room.'

Familiar with it? All she could see was the enormous carved bed heaped with pillows, and her imagination immediately stripped Andreas bare and pictured him sliding with that masculine grace she'd never seen on another man between the navy satin sheets.

She clenched her teeth together, trying to blink the image away and pretend the rush of blood she could feel pumping around her was not connected to it.

She'd never imagined a man naked before and it disturbed her that she should have such unwelcome thoughts about this particular man.

There was such a sensuous potency about him. It was there in his every move, his every breath, his every word, and all it did was add to her growing sense of danger.

Sheesh, she really, *really* needed some sleep.

'What other staff work here?' she asked. Once she knew where everyone was she would stop feeling as if she'd been trapped in a gilded cage that only Andreas had the key to.

Everything had happened so quickly and smoothly that day that there hadn't been time for her misgivings to do more than squeak at her but now, here, standing in Andreas's bedroom in his secret home in the middle of the night, those misgivings were shouting loudly.

'I inherited most of the staff from the previous owners. The grounds are managed by Enrique and his eldest son. Enrique's wife Sheryl and a couple of her friends take care of all the cleaning. Between them they know everything there is to know about the house and the peninsular and the Seychelles itself.'

'Where are the staff quarters?'

'There aren't any. Brendan and his assistant live in a cottage on the grounds but the others all live on the main island.'

Another chime of alarm rang in her ears. 'So who actually lives in the house?'

Surely she had misunderstood something. Surely she wouldn't be the only person living under this roof with him while they were there?

'We do. You and me.'

'*Just* you and me?'

'Yes.' His eyes seemed to do more than merely sparkle. They *smouldered*. His nostrils flared as he added, 'While we're on this beautiful spot of paradise, the night time belongs to you and me alone.'

CHAPTER THREE

ANDREAS ENJOYED CARRIE'S attempt to hide her horror at this clearly unwelcome revelation.

'I bought this place as a getaway from the world so it's run in a more relaxed way than my other homes,' he said. 'As long as I have someone close at hand to take care of my needs, I don't need much else and that, *matia mou*, is why you are here. Consider it an easy breaking-in for you. The house runs itself so you can dedicate your time here to me and we can get to know each other properly in the process.'

The colour drained from her face, her hazel eyes widening.

Understandable, he thought lazily. Carrie wouldn't want him delving into her life with probing questions that would put her on the spot. She wouldn't want to trip herself up with easily forgotten lies.

He admired that, through the tumult of emotions flickering through her eyes, her composure didn't waver. If he were ignorant of her true identity he doubted he would have noticed anything amiss. If he didn't know the truth he would assume she was a naturally quiet, self-contained woman.

He looked forward to seeing how far he could push her before she cracked and the real Carrie emerged.

'Now for your room. You will find it adequately appointed.' But not as adequately as Rochelle's had been. She was being put in a much different room from the one his former Domestic PA had enjoyed. Rochelle's room had been located at the other end of the house so she could have her privacy.

He didn't intend for Carrie, this cuckoo in his nest, this spy, to have any privacy during her interlude in his life. Her duties would be of the kind he would never dream of imposing on a proper employee.

Andreas turned the handle of a door in the middle of the left-hand wall of his room. It opened into a much smaller, adjoining room.

He spread a hand out. 'See? You have everything you need. A bed, a dressing table, wardrobe and your own bathroom.' But no television or other form of entertainment. Andreas intended to be Carrie's only source of entertainment while she was here.

The colour that stained her cheeks this time was definitely of the angry variety but she kept it in check to ask with only the slightest tremor, 'My room adjoins yours?'

'How would you take care of my needs if you were on the other side of the house? The previous owners used this room as a nursery. I admit it's rather small—it was designed for a small child before they went into a proper room of their own—but I can assure you it's perfectly adequate.' Adequate for a baby or toddler. Barely adequate for a fully grown woman, even one as slender as Carrie. He'd intended to turn it into another dressing room and was glad he hadn't got around to organising it.

'Where's the lock?'

'There isn't one so it will be nice and easy for you to come and go between our rooms.' He winked. 'But do not worry. I am a gentleman and only enter a lady's bedroom when invited.'

And should she be tempted to enter his room without invitation, which she undoubtedly would seeing as her whole purpose for being here was to snoop, then the microscopic cameras he'd had installed in his bedroom and throughout the house would monitor her every movement.

He'd intended to bug her room too with voice-activated cameras but had talked himself out of it. There was a line a person should never cross and bugging a lady's bedroom, even a journalistic spy like this one, was firmly on the wrong side of it. Now that he'd spent the day in such close confines to her, he was doubly glad he hadn't crossed that line.

Carrie had an allure about her that played to his senses like a finely tuned violin.

She also had eyes that looked bruised from exhaustion.

'I can see you're tired. Is there anything you wanted to ask before we retire for the night?'

She shook her head, those soft, plump lips drawing in together. The situation had clearly overwhelmed her. He could sympathise. When she had walked into his offices in the heart of London's financial district that morning she could not have guessed she'd finish the day cut off from everything she was familiar with in the paradise that was the Seychelles. No doubt she was feeling vulnerable.

Good.

He *could* sympathise but he would not. Carrie was a vulture. A beautiful vulture for sure, but a vulture nonetheless.

She deserved nothing less than what was coming for her.

'In that case, I bid you goodnight. The clothes I promised you were flown in while we were travelling. Sheryl has put them away for you. You will find them imminently suitable. And remember...'

A pretty brow rose cautiously. 'Remember?'

He winked. 'I like to be welcomed with a smile.'

As he closed the interconnecting door he smiled himself to imagine her reaction to the clothing selected for her.

His fun with Carrie was only just beginning.

Carrie threw the entire contents of her new wardrobe onto the narrow excuse of a bed and rifled through them with increasing anxiety.

She'd expected to be given outfits akin to what chambermaids in hotels wore, not clothing like this.

Her wardrobe and dresser had been filled with soft, floaty summer dresses, vest tops, shorts that put the meaning into the word 'short', bikinis and sarongs. There was underwear too, all of the black, lacy variety.

Every item had a designer label.

Her skin had never felt so heated as when she'd picked up a pair of knickers and wondered if Andreas had chosen them personally.

But how could he have done? She hadn't left his side since she'd stepped into his office. It must have been his PA, Debbie, who she'd been certain hadn't liked her in the initial interview and who she'd had to give her vital statistics to as Andreas had whisked her out of his building.

Carrie tugged at her hair with a mixture of consternation and fear.

Whoever had chosen the items, which included beach paraphernalia along with all the clothing, this was not right, not by any stretch of the imagination. To make matters worse there was no Internet she could connect to and her phone signal seemed to be non-existent. The text message she'd written to her editor forty minutes ago was still trying to send.

Who knew she was here? Andreas and his PA Debbie, his flight crew and his Seychellois domestic staff. No one from her own life knew she was in the Seychelles, only people employed by Andreas.

Rubbing her eyes, she told herself she was probably worrying over nothing. It had been an incredibly long day and she was sleep deprived. Sleep deprivation did funny things to the brain.

The letter inviting her to the second interview *had* stated the successful applicant would be expected to start the job immediately. It was her own fault that she hadn't taken the letter literally enough.

She was exactly where she wanted to be, with

greater access to the man than in her wildest dreams.

But he also had access to her, and she eyed the adjoining unlocked door with nerves fluttering in her chest.

There was no way she would trust his word that he wouldn't enter her room uninvited.

The way he looked at her... Did he look at all his employees with that same intensity? Did he leave the rest of his employees feeling that he was stripping them bare with a glance?

Or was it just her guilty conscience playing at her and making her see things that weren't there?

Movement from the adjoining room made her catch her breath.

Andreas was still awake. They were connected to each other's rooms and she couldn't even lock herself away from him.

She forced herself to breathe.

She needed to take a shower but had been holding it off until she could be reasonably sure he'd gone to sleep. An hour after he'd left her in this tiny bedroom, there was nothing to suggest he was ready to turn in.

What was he going to do? she chided herself. Walk in on her while she showered?

Sexual foibles were the easiest secrets to uncover. Andreas Samaras might be many things but a sex pest was not something that had been flagged up about him, not even on the secret grapevine from which she and other journalists like her got so many of their stories. He rarely dated and when he did it was discreetly. If there was anything along those lines she had to worry about she would already know about them.

She was being over-cautious when she didn't need to be.

Carefully putting the expensive clothing back into its rightful place, she realised what her real problem with it was. These were the sort of clothes a man bestowed on his lover for a holiday, not his employee.

Carrie awoke in the unfamiliar tiny room minutes before the digital alarm clock on her bedside table went off. It had been set for her by some faceless person that she would no doubt meet shortly, a person with whom she would have to pretend to be someone she was not.

Lying on an investigation had never bothered her before. The few she had done before, though, had been office-based. Offices were places where *everyone* wore a mask. She'd fitted in without any problems and without any guilt, knowing she was working for a good cause.

This was different. This was Andreas's home.

She had told herself over and over that this was an opportunity that had been gift-wrapped for her but she still felt as if she'd breached an invisible line.

He deserves it, she told herself grimly, focussing her mind on Violet's scarred, emaciated body and its root cause. *He deserves everything he gets.*

She checked her phone and sighed to see the message to her editor still pending. Her room must be in a black spot.

After a quick shower under the disappointing trickle of water in her private bathroom, only mitigated by the expensive, wonderfully scented toiletries provided for her, it was time to select an outfit to wear.

After rifling through her new clothing for the dozenth time she chose a dark blue dress covered in tiny white dots. It was made of the sheerest material, had the thinnest of spaghetti straps and fell to mid-thigh but at least it covered her cleavage. And, she had to admit, it *was* pretty.

Scrabbling through her handbag, she found a hairband wedged in the bottom and tied her hair into a loose bun at the nape of her neck. She had no make-up with her. Usually that didn't matter as she rarely wore it but today she felt she could do with some camouflage.

Dressed and feeling much more alert, she pulled the floor-length curtains open and gasped.

The sight that greeted her could have come from a postcard.

If she'd peeked through the curtains during the night she would have seen her room had its own private balcony. She stepped out onto it now, heart thumping, the sun kissing her skin good morning.

She closed her eyes to savour the feeling then opened them again, hand on her throat, staring in stunned awe at the deep blue sky unmarred by so much as a solitary cloud and at the stunning azure ocean that lapped gently onto the finest white sand imaginable, the cove's shore lined with palm trees. A short distance ahead sat an isolated green landmass that looked, from her dazed estimation, close enough that she might tread through water to it. An artist couldn't have painted a more perfect scene.

'Good morning, Caroline.'

The deep, cheerful voice startled her and she gripped the balustrade before turning her head.

So mind-blown had she been by the view before her, she hadn't noticed her balcony was far too wide to be hers alone.

Hair damp and wearing nothing but a pair of low-slung black shorts, Andreas strolled to stand beside her and grinned. 'What did I tell you about the view in daylight—takes the breath away, doesn't it?'

Her grip on the balustrade tightening, she stared back out at the view and nodded. 'It's stunning.'

But it was the view standing feet away from her that had truly stolen her breath and, though she tried her hardest to keep her attention on what lay in front of her, her senses were leaping to what stood beside her.

His body was even better than her imagination had allowed her to believe. Broad shouldered, muscular without being overdone and deeply tanned, this was a body kept fit by plenty of swimming and enjoyment of the outside life, not by lifting weights or working on a treadmill. This wasn't a body that had been sculptured out of vanity.

'Sleep well?' he murmured, resting his arms on the balustrade.

She inhaled and gave a sharp nod, intensely aware of his penetrative gaze on her.

So much for sleep curing her inexplicable awareness of him.

'Fine, thank you.'

'Good. Ready to start work?'

She nodded again.

'Then let's introduce you to the others and

get some breakfast. I don't know about you but I'm starving.'

'Okay.' She turned to go back into her room.

'Caroline?'

She met his sparkling gaze. 'Yes?'

'Have you forgotten my most basic requirement?'

She furrowed her brow as she tried to clear her mind of his semi-nakedness enough to think, pretended her insides hadn't just clenched and heated to see the fine dark hair that lightly covered his chest snaked down and over his hard abdomen to where his shorts rested low...

He shook his head in amusement. 'Where is my smile?'

'Still waking up,' she replied without thinking.

His grin was wide enough to eclipse the rising sun. 'Ah, you *do* have a sense of humour. I did wonder. Now let's get some breakfast.'

And with that, he strolled back into his room.

Carrie was on the brink of laughter for reasons she couldn't begin to understand, although she suspected it would have a hysterical quality to it if it came out, when clarity suddenly came to her.

She was *here*.

She'd got the job.

Everything was in place to allow her to do

what she'd spent the last three years dreaming of doing. The last thing she wanted was to blow the opportunity by not performing as required and getting sacked before she'd properly started.

Whatever strange reactions Andreas provoked inside her, she had to ignore them and do her job.

He'd made his requirements crystal clear. She was to be good humoured and cater to all his whims. Well, she would do just that. She would do everything he required of her *and* she would make darned sure to keep a smile on her face while she did it. She would inveigle her way into his confidence and uncover the secrets Andreas Samaras kept hidden from the world.

And then she would expose them.

And then, finally, she would find some peace of mind. Violet would have been avenged and both the men who'd destroyed her life would, in a much different way, be destroyed too.

With that happy thought in her head, she hurried to join him.

Breakfast had been laid out on the sunny veranda, an array of breads, pastries, fruits, condiments and yogurt.

'I take my coffee black without sugar,' Andreas said as he took his seat.

He'd introduced Carrie to his staff but had

kept it quick. He'd taken Enrique and Sheryl into his confidence and they'd been outraged to discover an investigative journalist was trying to infiltrate his life. They were honest, upstanding people who he knew would struggle to hide their true feelings towards her for any length of time.

He liked to think he was an honest man too, but dealing with the shysters and scumbags that littered the financial world he inhabited like the dregs of a pot of coffee had taught him how to play the game that the people he employed on this island could never understand.

Carrie, still standing, poured his coffee for him. She even poured it with a smile.

'I will have honeydew melon and yogurt,' he told her.

She took a bowl and, with another smile, spooned chunks of melon into it. 'Tell me when to stop.'

Her disposition since he'd startled her on the balcony had changed considerably, and very much for the better. He would bet her new, cheerful disposition was external only.

He waited until the bowl was full before raising a hand. He noticed her own hand was incredibly slim, the nails long and nicely shaped. If Carrie were to look at the hands of any of his domestic staff she would see none of them had nails as well maintained as hers. She would see her nails were a dead giveaway that her life had not been spent undertaking domestic work.

'Four spoonfuls of yogurt,' he commanded amiably.

Again, she obeyed. 'Can I get you anything else to go with it?'

Tempted though he was to ask her to spoon it into his mouth, just to see if the smile fixed on her face cracked, he resisted. 'That will do for the moment. I will let you know when I want anything else.'

She nodded and folded her hands together over her belly.

Andreas put a spoonful into his mouth and took the opportunity to cast his eyes over her again in an appreciative open manner he would never dream of doing with an ordinary employee.

She was a little smaller than the average woman, the modest dress she'd selected showcasing the lithe legs of a model and breasts he would never have guessed could be so full on so slight a person. The morning sunlight beamed on her face highlighting the soft dewiness of her skin, reflecting off her complexion in glimmering waves.

Carrie didn't need make-up. She was stunning exactly as she was.

It was fortuitous that she wasn't a proper employee of his, he thought, as a thick heaviness pooled in his loins. Boss-employee relationships were disasters waiting to happen and he steered well clear of them, just as he avoided anything that could harm his business and personal reputation. In today's climate, where sexual harassment charges were a mere compliment about a pretty outfit away, he was too conscious of his position and power to risk his reputation.

Carrie would be a challenge to his self-imposed ideals. If he had to work with her in a close environment for real he knew he would find it a challenge to keep their relationship on a professional footing, a notion he found faintly disturbing.

Here and under these unique circumstances, his personal ethics could be safely pushed aside. She wasn't his employee. She was a snake. A beautiful, beguiling, incredibly sexy snake who wanted to destroy him.

'Are you not going to sit down?' he asked once he'd swallowed his mouthful.

Her hazel eyes flickered, her brow furrowed slightly, but the smile stayed in place.

'Are you not intending to eat?'

Now the furrow in her brow deepened.

'I dislike eating alone, *matia mou*. While we're here it is my wish that you dine with me, so, please, sit. Pour yourself a drink and eat something.'

As she complied with his request, he couldn't resist adding, 'Also, if you dine with me, it makes it easier for you to wait on me.'

'Whatever makes your life easier,' she said demurely and with only a hint of teeth being ground together. 'I am here to serve you.'

'That you are,' he agreed. 'And you look beautiful doing it. Are you happy with the clothes selected for you?'

Her spoon, which had been adding a little yogurt into the bowl she'd taken for herself, hovered in her hand. 'Yes. Thank you. Although... I thought I would be given more...practical clothing.'

Poor Carrie. How disconcerting it must have been for her to open her wardrobe and find there was no uniform to hide behind, no means to slip unobtrusively into the shadows of his life.

'Practical clothing has no place in such a beautiful setting.'

'Well, it's very generous of you. I'm amazed you were able to get it all here before we arrived,' she said lightly.

'It's a bespoke Internet service my niece uses. She holidayed here during her Christmas break but flew over on a commercial flight and lost her luggage. Twelve hours later she had a whole new designer wardrobe delivered.' He gave a rueful laugh. 'I did wonder if Natalia lost her suitcase deliberately just so I could buy her new clothing.'

Carrie's face pinched in on itself as he spoke his niece's name but only briefly. If he hadn't been watching her so closely he would have missed it.

It was good to know she was squirming inside.

'Anyway, with all this talk of clothes, I should tell you that you will need to change after we've eaten,' he said.

'Why?'

'The current on my beach is too strong to swim in at this time of year but there's a cove on Tortue Island that's perfect. We will take my boat out there and swim and get to know each other better. Doesn't that sound good?'

Her throat moved before she nodded and smiled. 'I can't think of anything I'd like more.'

CHAPTER FOUR

IF THE WIND CHANGED, Carrie was quite sure her face would freeze with this pathetic smile stuck on it for ever. Her cheeks ached with the effort of it and all she wanted was for the slave-driving Greek egomaniac to let her go to bed and get away from him for some respite.

She'd thought the day before had been long… It had *nothing* on the day she'd just endured, which, despite being late evening, showed no sign of ending soon.

Tortue Island had been the tiny green island paradise she'd spotted from her balcony, a mere five-minute hop on Andreas's speedboat. He'd taken her to a secluded cove surrounded by enormous palm trees and drenched in sunlight. That was where paradise had ended.

Violet as a toddler had been easier to take care of than this overgrown infant. Practically the only thing she hadn't had to do for Andreas was towel him dry after his frequent swims.

She'd kept him supplied with constant refreshments, opened his bottles of water, peeled his fruit, fanned him when he'd decided he was too hot, even read news articles off his tablet for him, which had been financial articles and as exciting to read as it was to watch paint dry.

And she'd had to do it all with a cheerful demeanour!

The only thing that had kept her cheerful was imagining his smug face when he discovered her true identity. He'd mentioned that they would be flying back to London before heading on to Frankfurt and she couldn't *wait* to get going. Both of those homes had proper offices set up for him to work from—he was so lazy she was surprised he bothered having offices outside his homes—and she just knew it wouldn't take her long to discover his illegal secrets.

She couldn't get over how spoilt and lazy he was. If someone had told her the rugged Andreas Samaras liked to have his grapes peeled for him as if he were a Roman emperor, she would never have believed it, and she had applied for a job with him with the lowest expectations of the man. It just didn't fit with what she thought she knew of him. But, no, he clearly adored being waited on, a wolfish smile near enough constantly playing on his lips.

Once he'd grown bored of Tortue Island, they'd returned to his peninsular where Carrie had waited on him some more while he'd sunbathed by his swimming pool.

She had never imagined a man like Andreas could do so much sunbathing!

Her duties at the pool had consisted mostly of sitting by his side with a handheld fan aimed at his face in between runs to his fully stocked poolside bar for ever more refreshments for him. Then it had been time to prepare his clothing for dinner and take a super-quick shower herself before they went to sit out on his veranda for their evening meal. Other than her shower, she hadn't had a minute to herself, had only been able to check for a phone signal as she'd chucked a clean dress on after her super-quick shower. No magical signal had been found; her text message still sat pending.

The meal cooked for them by Brendan had been possibly the best food she'd ever tasted, fat succulent tiger prawn salad—Andreas had got her to shell his prawns for him—followed by a creamy coconut curry, but she'd been unable to appreciate it as Andreas had had her running back and forth to the kitchen like a yo-yo.

She hadn't done so much exercise in years.

'Caroline?'

She suddenly realised that while she'd been

silently fuming about his lazy, slave-driving ways, he'd been speaking to her.

She fixed the wide smile back on her face.

What do you want this time? Another bowl of water set at the optimum temperature to dip your fingers into? Another napkin to dry them with or to wipe your mouth to go with the five I've already had to get for you?

'Sorry, I missed what you said.'

He drained his white wine and set the glass on the table. 'I'm ready to go in...'

About time.

'...so I need you to run me a bath and turn my bed down.'

'Turn your bed down?' she answered blankly, not having the faintest idea what he was talking about.

His forehead creased and he tilted his head. 'You've never turned a bed down before?'

Sensing danger, she hid her apprehension with a smile. 'It's not something that's been asked of me before. Maybe I know it by another name?'

'I thought it was a universal term.' A suggestive gleam sparkled in his eyes. 'It just means preparing my bed so it's ready for me—turning the sheets over so I can slide into them.'

'Oh, *that*,' she said with feigned brightness. Yes, this was exactly the sort of thing this spoilt man would demand. She would bet that in colder climates he would demand his domestic PA personally warm his bed for him. 'Of course. Yes. Anything else?'

'I'll let you know if anything comes to mind while you're running my bath.'

I just bet you will.

She got to her feet. 'I'll run it for you now. What temperature do you like it?' Scalding or ice-cold? she prevented herself from asking.

He waited a beat before answering, a smile tugging on his lips. 'Why don't you run it to the temperature *you* like?'

Andreas watched Carrie walk into the house to run him a bath with amusement fizzing in his veins.

He couldn't remember the last time he'd enjoyed himself as much as he had that day.

She waited on him as if she'd been born to serve his whims. Her determination to act the role he'd set for her and act it well had been exquisite to watch.

The little tells that had betrayed her real feelings had been equally exquisite. When this was all over he'd have to arrange for her to be given an acting award because he was quite certain he would never have seen those betraying signs if he hadn't been looking for them.

When this was all over…

That was a thought to knock the smile from his face.

He would have to put Carrie out of her misery sooner rather than later, however enjoyable it was to play the role of spoilt playboy, a role that, despite his riches, he'd never had the time or inclination to play before. With Carrie being the one to act the role of slave, the spoilt playboy role had been one to relish. What a shame he would have to put a stop to it so soon.

Debbie had messaged him earlier with news that made it clear he needed to return to London and start on damage limitation. Whatever Carrie's reasons for being here, she'd prodded a hornets' nest.

He poured himself another glass of wine. Other than shave, it was the first thing he'd done for himself all day. He took a sip, leaned back and closed his eyes.

His graduation from university had coincided with his parents' world falling apart. Since then, his life had been one long conveyor belt of obligations. Family, work, responsibility, with Andreas the one holding everyone and everything together. Then, as he'd seen light at the end of the long dark tunnel, his sister and brother-in-law had died and he'd suddenly found himself guardian to his teenage niece. Natalia had been raised in London and was already a weekly boarder at her school in the English capital when her parents died. Andreas hadn't wanted to uproot her life any further so had uprooted himself instead, moving his life and business from Manhattan to London. Natalia had become his priority.

He had never begrudged anything he'd done for his family. It was what families did—they loved and took care of each other. But it was only when Natalia had left for university and he'd felt the burden of responsibility lifting from his shoulders that he'd realised what a weight it had been on him. That weight had been there most of his adult life.

Now Natalia was approaching the end of her first year at university, that flicker of light beckoning his freedom he'd seen before her parents had died was flickering again, brighter than it ever had before. Technically Natalia was now an adult. She still needed him but not in the way she had before. Nowadays she only needed his money and his London home to 'crash' in, as she put it, when she went out partying with friends in the city. She was young, working hard and enjoying her life, exactly as she should be.

He'd promised himself that once she'd completed her first year he would start living his life for himself. He no longer had to worry about being a good influence or role model. He could enjoy the wealth he had created and experience what life had to offer but which responsibility had denied him for so long.

He never wanted to have any form of responsibility in his personal life ever again.

His business, though, was a different matter entirely and it was this he vowed to protect from Carrie Rivers's poisonous pen.

He drank some more of his wine and reflected that it was fortuitous that Carrie had set her sights on him when he had the freedom to do whatever was needed to stop her. Whisking her to the Seychelles would have been unthinkable a year ago when he'd still planned every minute of his life around Natalia's schedule.

Setting his empty glass on the table, he got to his feet, rolled his neck and stretched.

He would hit Carrie with the truth in the morning. Until then, he intended to extract his last few hours of fun from her.

Carrie marched into Andreas's bathroom, switched the light on and stopped short.

Soft lighting revealed a space that wasn't a bathroom but a marble palace. The walk-in shower alone was bigger than her bathroom.

But it was the deep, sunken bath she approached, as opulent as anything Roman emperors had bathed in. Half a dozen people could fit in it with room to spare.

It took her a few moments to work out where the plug was. Then she turned the taps on. A surge of water gushed out, not just from the taps but from tiny round holes the entire circumference, all pouring quicker than she had ever known water to pour before.

She found bath foam in a cabinet and added a liberal dollop, which immediately filled the room with a delicious warm spicy scent, then adjusted the water temperature some more, resisting the urge to set it on cold. When the bath was run and filled with thick foam, she dried her hands and went back into his bedroom.

Her bravado almost deserted her as she approached his bed.

She'd been in his room a number of times that day but this was the first time she'd had to go near his bed.

She took a deep breath before carefully untucking the sheet. She pulled it back to form a triangle, then smoothed it, trying not to think that only the night before these sheets had covered his naked body.

Because he did sleep naked. She knew that on an instinctive level she couldn't begin to understand and the mere thought made her lower abdomen clench tightly.

You've had too much sun, she told herself grimly, lifting his pillow to plump and immediately releasing Andreas's scent trapped in the Egyptian cotton. She hurriedly put the pillow back down as the scent entered her bloodstream and, for a moment, her pulses soared with such strength she felt dizzy.

She blinked hard to regain her focus and stared at the pillow as if it could bite her.

'Is my bath ready?'

She jumped.

Andreas stood at the threshold of his bedroom, a wry smile playing on his lips.

How long had he been there, watching her...?

'Yes. There's fresh towels on the rail. Everything's ready for you.' How she managed to get the words out with her heart thrashing so wildly and leaping in her throat she didn't know.

'Good.' He stepped into the room, eyes on her as he removed a cufflink from the sleeve of his shirt.

Suddenly terrified that he was going to strip in front of her, she forced her legs to move towards the door to her own room, sidestepping around his huge figure, which somehow seemed even taller and broader than it did in daylight hours.

'I could do with some water,' he said as her hand touched the door handle. 'Can you bring a glass up for me please?'

A please? That was a first.

Carrie nodded tightly and hurried out of his room, down the stairs and to the kitchen, resolutely telling herself over and over that she'd had far too much sun that day and that was why her veins were fizzing so. The young kitchen assistant was just finishing for the night, a reminder that very soon the house would be empty of everyone but her and Andreas...

All she could hope was that this was her last duty of the evening.

Her heart still hammered frantically as she walked back up the stairs with his glass of water.

His bedroom door was ajar. She knocked lightly on it. When there was no response she stepped tentatively inside. His room was empty, the bathroom door wide open.

'I have your water,' she called. 'Shall I leave it on the table for you?'

His reply was muffled by the thick walls. 'I'll have it in here.'

Hoping she'd misheard him, she confirmed, 'What, in the bathroom?'

'Seeing as that's where I am, yes.'

Taking a deep, fortifying breath, Carrie trod slowly to the open door, praying he hadn't removed all his clothes yet.

It was a futile hope.

Andreas was in the huge bath, leaning back,

the top of his chest right in her eyeline, facing the door. Facing her.

Knowing her face had gone the colour of sun-ripened tomatoes, she looked everywhere but him, searching for a decent spot to put the glass on.

'Bring it to me,' he commanded casually.

She couldn't get her feet to work.

Water sloshed as he sat up and extended an arm. 'Don't be shy, *matia mou*. I only bite if invited to.'

Flames engulfing her, resisting the urge to throw the water right in his face, she finally put one foot in front of the other, her eyes darting everywhere but at him.

She *couldn't* look at him, not directly. As long as she looked at the beautiful cream tiling around his head she would be fine.

When she reached his side she extended her own arm to put the glass in his waiting hand, careful not to allow their fingers to brush, then quickly stepped back.

'I'll leave you to enjoy your bath,' she said.

'You're not going to stay and keep me company?'

Without her meaning them to, her eyes found his and her heart leapt then twisted.

A breathless, suspended moment passed between them, the only movement the growing ache in her most feminine place and the colour she could feel creeping up her neck.

And no wonder she couldn't breathe. The look in his eyes… The gleam…

This beautiful, ruggedly handsome man was staring at her as if she were a delicacy he wanted to feast on.

Heat rose in her that she was quite sure had nothing to do with the steamy vapours coming from the bath.

Suddenly her imagination ran riot, a feast of its own, racing into places she had never been before of naked limbs and soft sighs…

She'd spent the whole day with this man's semi-naked body within touching distance and had successfully kept him fully clothed in her mind, just as if she'd been a subject in *The Emperor's New Clothes*. Blocking out his near-nakedness had been as hard as keeping that stupid smile on her face but she had done it. Now the veil she'd put over her eyes had been ripped away and she saw *him*, darkly tanned, a homage to rugged masculinity, and the base feminine part of herself responded to it.

And then she saw something else in his eyes, something darker even than the desire that swirled and pulsed, and it was this something, this dark danger, that pulled her out of the hypnotic spell he'd cast over her and snapped her back to herself.

She forced herself to breathe and dragged her lips into a smile.

'You're a big boy,' she said in as light a tone as she could muster. 'I'm sure you can cope with your own company for a while.'

There was a moment of utter stillness before his firm lips curved into an all too knowing smile. 'I didn't think you'd looked.'

Looked…?

Suddenly his meaning became clear and her eyes, with a will of their own, gazed down at the water, at the long, muscular legs laid out, covered in foam but not covered enough that she couldn't see the dark hair between his thighs or his…

Shocked rigid, she quickly blinked and turned away.

But she couldn't blink enough to rid herself of what she'd seen.

She'd never seen a fully naked man before, not in the flesh, and, even with the bath water and foam distorting the image, she didn't need to be experienced in matters of the flesh to know that he was in proportion *everywhere*.

'I'll be in my room if you need me,' she mumbled, hurrying to escape from this seductive atmosphere and all the danger lacing it.

She closed the bathroom door with the sound of his low laughter ringing in her ears.

Alone in her bedroom she sat on her bed and clutched her still-flaming cheeks, breathing heavily.

She despised Andreas, had hated him from that moment outside the headmistress's office when he had stared at her as if she were something dirty he had trodden in.

He had destroyed her sister!

How could she feel such attraction to him? How was it possible that her first real flush of desire should be for her enemy?

And how was it possible that he could be so aware of it? She'd seen it in those seductive eyes…

She flopped onto her pillow face-first and gave a muffled scream.

How could she be thinking these thoughts?

Too much sun.

Of *course*. That was the answer.

She'd had more sun in one day than she'd had for at least three years. It had addled her brain in much the same way sleep deprivation had addled it yesterday.

Feeling calmer, she stretched herself out on the narrow bed, closed her eyes and concentrated on inhaling and exhaling in long, regular breaths, the way she had long ago trained her-

self to fall asleep when her terrified fears for
her sister had threatened to stop her ever falling into oblivion.

A loud rapping woke Carrie from the light slum-
ber she had fallen into.

The digital bedside clock showed it had just
turned midnight. She'd been in her room for
less than an hour.

The rapping vibrated through the door again.
'Caroline?'

'I'm awake.' She staggered off the bed and took
the one step needed to reach the door, straightening her dress, which she'd fallen asleep in.

She braced herself before opening the door
only to find her senses hit immediately with the
tangy scent of Andreas's cologne and the faint
spice of his bath foam.

He was standing in a pair of faded jeans, his
torso bare, a smile playing on his lips.

'Were you sleeping?' he asked with one eye-
brow raised.

'Dozing.' *I forgot that working for you meant
only sleeping when you gave the order.*

'Good. I'm in the mood for a nightcap.'
Of course you are.

'You want me to get it for you?'

He pulled a face that said very clearly that
that was what he employed her for.

'Give me a second to put something on my feet,' she added hastily.

'Bring me a tumbler of Scotch—any single malt will do—three fingers, two cubes of ice, and one for yourself. I'll be on the veranda.' Then he winked, turned and headed off.

Taking a deep breath while internally cursing him to the heavens, Carrie slipped her toes into the gold designer flip-flops she'd been given and trudged down the stairs to his den, where he kept his indoor bar.

How could any normal self-respecting employee put up with this? she wondered. No salary, however large, could compensate for being at Andreas's permanent beck and call.

She fixed his Scotch exactly as demanded and poured herself some lemonade. As tempting as the vast array of liquors and spirits was, she didn't want any alcohol in her bloodstream when dealing with this tricky man. She'd refused wine with her dinner for the same reason.

She carried the glasses outside, where a fresh breeze whispered over her skin, and found him back at the outside table reading something on his phone.

She still didn't have a signal.

His teeth glimmered white in the moonlight as she put the drinks on the table. 'Before you sit down, go to my dressing room and get me a pair of swim-shorts. I might want a swim later.'

Later? It was already the middle of the night. Did the man not plan on getting *any* sleep?

Was *she* not allowed to get any sleep?

Then she caught something in his eyes, an amusement that immediately aroused her suspicions...

Was he...?

Could he be...?

Was Andreas playing a *game*?

He stared right back at her, the amusement no longer just in his eyes but quirking on his lips, as if he were biting back laughter. But something darker lurked in those light brown eyes too, something that sent fresh alarm bells ringing inside her.

She backed away slowly, suddenly wary of taking her eyes off him.

Her job had taught her the importance of listening to her instincts and her instincts were telling her loud and clear that something was off and that some unseen danger awaited her.

Climbing back up the stairs, she realised that she'd had this instinctual feeling of something being amiss since her interview with him but Andreas had kept her so busy running around after him that she'd had no time to listen.

She paused at the threshold of his bedroom

and gazed around with narrowed eyes. She'd resisted looking too deeply before as there had always been someone around and she hadn't wanted to seem as if she were doing anything other than what Andreas was supposedly paying her for. The newest members of staff in any organisation always attracted curious glances, whether the work was in a business or domestic environment. It was human nature to watch strangers more closely than people you were familiar with. She'd thought it wise to hold off before she started any snooping.

Slowly she took all the expensive furnishings in, unsure what, if anything, she was looking for.

It was just a bedroom. A masculine, richly opulent bedroom for sure, but still, just a bedroom...

What the heck was *that*?

Right at the end of the curtain pole that covered his French doors, a tiny round object winked at her.

Carrie had been an undercover journalist long enough to know exactly what she was looking at but it still took a few moments before it really sank in.

The tiny round object was a camera. And it was filming her.

CHAPTER FIVE

ANDREAS SIPPED HIS Scotch as he watched Carrie on his phone.

He'd seen the suspicion in her eyes in the moments before she'd gone back inside to cater to his latest whim. Instinct had made him switch his phone over to the live feed coming from his bedroom.

Judging by the stillness in her frame as she stared around his bedroom, he suspected her own instincts had kicked in too.

After a couple of minutes of nothing, her expression suddenly changed, sharpening, her head tilting, brow furrowing as she walked trance-like towards the French door.

And then she was looking right at him...

Her pretty lips formed a perfect O as he watched realisation hit her.

Suddenly she was on the move, her face set, lips now pressed tightly together. She dragged a chair to the curtains and climbed onto it and yanked the camera out. The picture disappeared and he had to wait a few seconds for one of the others to kick in in its place. By then she'd found another, hidden in plain sight on the television. Her face now twisted with rage, she mouthed a curse at him before yanking that one out too.

She made her way systematically around the room until she'd removed all four hidden cameras and there were no more feeds left.

Andreas sipped more Scotch and prepared himself for the storm that was surely going to follow, breathing deeply to abate the weighty beats of his heart.

This was it, a few hours sooner than anticipated. Time for the truth to be revealed.

He didn't have to wait long.

The patio doors slammed open and Carrie appeared, marching straight towards him. When she reached the table, she snatched the glass from his hands and dropped the four tiny cameras into the Scotch.

He looked her up and down as she faced him, hands clenched in fists at her sides, chest heaving, her furious face pinched, looking ready to punch his lights out.

'Why don't you sit down?' he suggested coolly.

In many respects, it was better for the truth to come out now, when it was just the two of them and no witnesses.

Her lips parted and her jaw moved, clearly struggling to get any words out. When they finally came they were barely audible. 'You know, don't you?'

'That you're the undercover journalist Carrie Rivers?' He hooked an ankle on his thigh. 'Yes, *matia mou*, I know exactly who you are. I've always known.'

'So…this has all been a game?'

He allowed himself a smile. 'And what a game it has been. You have played it exquisitely. You make an excellent skivvy.'

She moved so quickly she was a blur, grabbing her glass and throwing the lemonade in his face.

Carrie, her heart a heavy burr, her stomach a mass of knots, fought for breath, feeling not the slightest bit of satisfaction to see the cold liquid soaking his face and hair.

He hadn't even flinched.

Of all the things she hated about him, at that moment the greatest thing to loathe was that he was sitting there, as cool as a cucumber with lemonade dripping off him while she couldn't even control her own breathing.

But then his eyes clashed with hers and she realised he wasn't as cool as he appeared. His jaw was taut and his eyes as dark as she'd ever seen them, filled to the brim with the danger she had always sensed but had stupidly chosen to ignore.

He'd known who she was all along. Right from the beginning.

Her brain burned just to recall it all. She'd *known* there was something wrong with the way he'd got her waiting on him hand and foot, had been too focussed on the prize at the end to allow herself to think about it. She'd also, she had to admit with painful humiliation, been too busy fighting her reactions to him to pay attention to all the dangers and warnings.

She'd ignored everything her instincts had been telling her.

It had all been a game and she had fallen for it.

She had infiltrated his life to bring him down but he had turned the tables on her and played her like a toy.

Slowly and deliberately, he wiped his sodden face with his hands and shook the liquid away, his piercing eyes never leaving her face.

'I believe it is time for you to tell me why you are really here, *Carrie Rivers*.'

His tone cut through her along with the words he used.

'But before you start, tell me your real name. Are you Carrie or Caroline? Or would you prefer I address you as Lying Snake?'

'I'm not the snake here.' Why did her voice have to tremble so much? 'How many cameras have you had spying on me?'

'Enough to have monitored your every move if the need had arisen.'

'You spied on me while I slept? While I...?' She shuddered, unable to voice her thoughts.

He must have read them though for he frowned. 'There were no cameras in your bedroom or any of the bathrooms. Unlike you, I have boundaries.'

'Boundaries?' she shouted. 'You had me bring you a drink while you were in the bath!'

'And didn't you enjoy looking at me?' he mocked. 'Now answer my question. Your real name.'

Cheeks burning, she glared at him, willing him to feel the hate vibrating out of her and to be scorched by it. Then she straightened her spine and spoke steadily. 'My legal name is Caroline Fiona Dunwoody, exactly as it says on my passport. I have been known as Caroline Rivers since my mother remarried when I was four but my name was never legally changed. I have always been called Carrie.'

'So, Caroline Dunwoody Rivers, why are you investigating me?'

She put her hands on her hips and glared at him. 'I'm not answering that.'

'You are,' he contradicted amiably. 'I promise that by the time the sun comes up you will have told me everything I wish to know.' He leaned forward. 'You are an award-winning journalist. You specialise in exposing the illegal practices of rich businessmen. You went to a lot of effort to infiltrate my life. You supplied false references. Debbie spoke to the people you stated were your referees. I assume these were your colleagues and that this sting has been carefully orchestrated by you and your newspaper. Investigations are not started on a whim. I want to know what started this whole ball rolling. I want to know *everything*.'

She listened to his words, delivered in such a reasonable tone but with steel lacing the staccato, with mounting fury at herself.

Why had she not listened to her instincts when she'd walked into his office and every nerve in her body had told her to turn on her heels and run?

And how was she supposed to answer any of his questions without dragging herself deeper into the hole she'd stupidly and unwittingly allowed herself to fall into?

When she remained tight-lipped, he sighed. 'Caroline...'

'Carrie.'

His broad shoulders raised nonchalantly. 'I

don't care. What I *do* care about is the truth and we're not going anywhere until you give me answers. You've lied and lied and now you owe me the truth.'

She put her hands on the table and glared at him. 'I don't owe you a damned thing and you lied too. You didn't have to go along with the pretence. You could have confronted me in the interview.'

'And have you run straight back to your newsroom and out of my reach?'

'But why have me skivvy after you? What was the point in that?'

'You really need to ask?' Amusement flared in the darkness of his eyes. 'You wanted to destroy me. The least I could do was let you suffer a little humiliation in return. I haven't enjoyed myself so much in years.' The amusement dropped. 'Someone is out to destroy me. It is either a business rival or a disgruntled ex-employee, or you are on a personal vendetta… because you and I have history, don't we, Carrie Rivers, sister of Violet?'

It was the way Carrie's face contorted at the mention of her sister's name that was the clincher for Andreas.

His intuition had been right all along. For Carrie, this was personal.

He got to his feet. 'Stay here. I'm going to get us a drink.'

'I don't want anything.'

'*I* do. And when I get back you will sit down and you will tell me everything because I promise you this—you won't be leaving the Seychelles until you do.'

He left her standing there, white-faced in her fury, and strode inside to his bar. He looked through the rows of bottles and plumped for a bottle of whisky, a brand with the spicy bite he needed right then.

Grabbing two crystal tumblers, he headed back to the veranda, part of him expecting Carrie to still be stubbornly standing where he'd left her but she'd sat down, legs crossed and arms folded across her chest, giving him what he could only describe as a death stare.

He took his seat opposite her, unscrewed the lid and poured them both a hefty measure. He pushed one of the tumblers to her. 'You're welcome to throw this in my face or smash the glass but it won't change anything.'

She picked it up with a scowl and sniffed it. 'It smells disgusting.'

'Don't drink it, then.'

She took a sip and pulled a face. 'It tastes worse than it smells.' That didn't stop her taking another sip.

He settled back and stared at her. She met his

gaze, the hazel of her eyes reflecting fire at him. The effect gave her beauty a majesty.

Whatever had motivated Carrie to set out to destroy him, she thought she had right on her side. She was set for a humiliating disappointment.

'Okay, let us establish some facts to begin with. The paper you work for has a reputation for excellent journalism and I include you in that. When it splashes on a big story the rest of the media follows. It is rarely sued for libel and when it is it rarely loses—namely, it backs up its stories. It is a serious, weighty newspaper. It doesn't print spurious gossip. It stands to reason that there was evidence for your editor or whoever is in charge of signing investigations off to think it worth their time and expense sending you to investigate me. What was that evidence?'

She dropped her gaze from his and took another sip of the whisky she professed to hate.

'The evidence?' he repeated, his patience waning.

'There were rumours.'

He drummed his fingers on the table. 'Rumours? About what?'

Her chin lifted. 'That you were embezzling your clients' funds.'

'What a pile of rubbish. Where did these rumours come from? Because I can assure you they are lies. Markets go up and down but I invest my clients' money with the same care I would if it were my own. I defy you to find a single investor who would say otherwise.'

Something flickered on her face, a shamed, guilty expression she tried to cover by taking a bigger sip of her whisky.

But it was too late. He'd seen it. Seen her guilt.

'The rumours came from you, didn't they? What did you do? Go to your editor and say you had a credible tip-off about me that was worth investigating?'

She lifted her head to look at him, her lips drawn tightly together. The truth was right there in her eyes.

He breathed deeply, trying to contain the anger swirling like a maelstrom in him. 'Come on, Carrie. It is just you and me. There is no one to hear what we say. We have both been playing games and now it is time for them to stop. Be honest and admit the truth. You went to your editor with a pack of lies about me, didn't you?'

Carrie's chest had compacted so tightly that she couldn't draw breath.

They'd both been playing games?

This had *never* been a game for her. This had been her sister's life, which Andreas had destroyed.

Everything she had done, the risks she had taken, the lies she had told, had all been for Violet and now she had to face that it had all been for nothing.

He'd rumbled her before she'd even set foot in his office and any secrets he had would remain secret.

She would never be able to expose him. Violet would never see justice.

Pulling air into her cramped lungs, she looked him square in the eyes. 'Yes.'

'Yes?'

'Yes. It was a pack of lies. I told my editor that I'd had a tip-off from a credible source that you were embezzling funds and, yes, he believed me.'

'He authorised your investigation into me on nothing more than your word?'

She leaned forward, willing him to feel every atom of her hate for him. 'I have spent three years dreaming about bringing you down and when the time came, there was no way I was going to let it slip through my fingers. Believe me, I was *very* convincing.'

'You have been plotting this for three years?' He shook his head slowly. 'I assume this has something to do with your screwed-up sister?'

His words cut through her like an arsenic-laced blade. 'Do not speak of Violet like that.'

Now he was the one to lean forward, close enough for her to see the stubble breaking out on his jaw. 'I have no idea what kind of a woman she's grown into but do not delude yourself as to what she was like three years ago. She was a mess.'

Carrie's rage consumed her so totally that it took what felt an age before she could speak. When she finally managed to get the words out, they tumbled from her, three years of pent-up heartbreak and anger spilling out in a torrent.

'Yes, Violet was a screwed-up mess. And do you know why? It was because *you* let your drug-peddling friend seduce her under your own roof. Between you and your bastard friend, you ruined her life, so yes, the reason I'm here *is* for Violet. I knew all I had to do was find a way into your life and I would find the evidence I needed to expose you as the monster you are and kill the squeaky-clean image you've fooled the world into believing.'

'What the *hell* are you talking about?'

Andreas had listened to the venom pouring from Carrie's tongue with growing incredulity and outrage. He'd suspected her motives were personal, that she had a grudge linked back to her sister's expulsion, but had assumed she had seized the opportunity to investigate and potentially expose him when the opportunity had come.

While he could take some relief that there was no business rival trying to blacken his name or anything nefarious going on within his company he was unaware of, it felt like ice in his veins to know he'd spent the past three years unaware he had such a dangerous enemy patiently biding her time and working against him.

'As if you don't know!' Putting her hands on the table, she rose to her feet like a phoenix emerging from the ashes, her face more animated and alive with colour than he could have believed. 'James Thomas. Violet met him when she was staying in your home, under your care. He groomed her—what teenager wouldn't be thrilled to have a rich, handsome man showering her with expensive gifts and attention? He bedded her for the first time on her sixteenth birthday, the clever, underhand bastard. He was *thirty-six*! They had a six-month affair and in that time he introduced her to drugs and all manner of perversions, and then he dumped her.

'When she refused to go quietly, he threatened to destroy her—five days later and drugs were found in her school bedside table and she was expelled, her life destroyed exactly as he'd promised. *You* instigated the search of her bedroom, *you*, his friend, and don't you dare deny it—the headmistress told me that you had informed her Violet and Natalia had been taking drugs and urged her to search their room. What an amazing coincidence that drugs were only found in Violet's possessions and only Violet was expelled. Your niece got off scot-free.'

Andreas took a deep breath, veering from rage to horror and back again, furious at the accusations being levelled at him but also revolted that Carrie—that anyone—could think him capable of covering up such depravity.

'Let me make one thing very clear,' he said levelly. 'James Thomas is no friend of mine and never has been. I knew nothing of this.'

'You would say that,' she scorned.

He downed his whisky before looking her in the eye. 'Be very careful, *matia mou*. I can see you are emotional right now but you have made many slanderous accusations against me and I *will* defend myself. James Thomas came to my home once, years ago, with a number of other potential investors for a business dinner. That is the only time I met him because I disliked him on sight and refused to take his business. I don't remember Violet being there that weekend but accept she could have been. I knew nothing of any affair between them.'

'If you weren't in cahoots with him—and I congratulate you on keeping your association with him out of the public eye—then why did you get Violet expelled?'

'Because I came home early from an evening out and discovered Violet and Natalia off their heads on drugs and alcohol. It was the weekend before her expulsion. Do you remember? Because I sure as hell do. That is a weekend I will never forget.'

The rage had turned to bewilderment. 'You caught them taking drugs?'

'Yes.'

'And you didn't think to tell me?'

'I would have called you in the morning but events took a turn that changed everything. After letting them know how disgusted I was with their behaviour, I sent them to bed to sleep it off and sober up. An hour later Violet came into my bedroom naked.'

'Liar.'

'I do not lie. In her intoxicated state she thought I was going to call the headmistress to warn her of what I had found. She thought seducing me would soften my anger and stop me reporting them. Violet had left cannabis and cocaine in her bedside table at school and knew it would be found if their room was searched and that she would be expelled. She was already on a final warning for disruptive behaviour as you know perfectly well.'

Carrie looked as if she were going to be sick.

She would look worse if he relayed how Violet had tried to climb into his bed and the filthy language she had used. He dreaded to think what kind of films she'd watched to imagine he would find such language a turn-on.

'I will spare you the details but Violet became hysterical when I rejected her. The noise woke Natalia. She tried to calm her and got a smack in the face from Violet for her trouble. If Violet hadn't been only sixteen I would have kicked her out onto the street. As it was, I waited until morning and sent her home in a cab.

'You are correct that I influenced Violet's expulsion. I make no apologies for it. Natalia confessed in the morning that Violet had been running wild and using drugs for months. Natalia was being drawn into a world she didn't know how to escape. That is what prompted me to call the school—I was protecting my niece. I am not in cahoots with James Thomas. I despise the man.'

As he'd been relating the sordid details, Carrie's face had turned ashen. She paced a few steps then spun around. 'Why didn't you tell me? If Violet tried to seduce you… If *any* of this is true…' Her eyes found his, censure merging with the bewilderment.

'I left it to the school to fill you in on what your sister had been up to.'

'The school…?' Fresh fury wiped the ashen complexion from her face. 'The headmistress didn't give us even two minutes of her time. All she told us was that drugs had been found in Violet's personal effects and that she was expelled. She kicked her out just like that.' She snapped her fingers for emphasis. 'You should have called me as soon as you found them. I was her guardian. I should have been told.'

Andreas hardened himself to the guilty feeling pooling in his stomach and rose to his feet, walking over to look her in the eye. 'After the stunt Violet pulled I wanted nothing more to do with either of you. If I am being honest I assumed she had learned her tricks from you…'

Almost too late he saw the hand come flying towards him and only just managed to snatch hold of the wrist before the fingers connected with his face.

CHAPTER SIX

HOLDING HER STRUGGLING wrist up in the air, Andreas stared into the furious hazel eyes. 'Let me finish. At the time I made the assumption she had learned to seduce a man through watching you, her older sister. That was my mistake and I apologise for it—I was angrier than I have ever been and incredibly worried for my niece, who told me the next morning that Violet had been in and out of different boys' beds for months. What would you have done in my position? What would you have done if it had been Natalia running wild and dragging Violet down with her?'

She'd stopped her struggle against his hold. For a moment the anger disappeared to be replaced with sadness. 'If it had been the other way round I would have told you. Violet needed help not condemnation. If I had been told then…' She sighed, seeming to deflate with the motion. 'It probably wouldn't have made any difference. The damage had already been done.

Violet *had* been sleeping around—the naïve fool thought it would make James jealous. She was desperate for him to take her back, totally unable to accept they were over, and she had no one to talk to about it. He'd made her keep it a secret and I think that screwed with her head as much as anything but she'd been completely under his spell. I only discovered the truth after the expulsion.'

And now, as she recalled the horror and despair she'd felt when Violet had made her confession, she felt the same guilt that she'd been so unaware that her darling baby sister had had an affair with a rich man old enough to be her father and who had fed her all the drugs she could consume.

Slowly it penetrated that Andreas's hold on her wrist had loosened and slid down to cover her hand. She shook it off and stepped back. She didn't want his sympathy.

Even with all the anger and hate that had flown between them there had still lived in Carrie a basic toxic awareness of him that her brain had no control over. Her hand zinged from his hold, causing a thrashing in her chest that echoed loudly in her ears.

She forced out a long breath and fought to think clearly.

She mustn't let his touch affect her thoughts.

But he didn't even need to touch her to make her react.

Moments ago she'd been inches from hitting him. She'd never hit anyone before, never even come close, and the violence she felt towards him terrified her as much as anything else.

When she next spoke, she did everything she could to keep her tone more moderate. 'Why did Violet say you set her up if it wasn't true? She was adamant about it. I took her home after that awful meeting with that condescending witch of a headmistress and she swore you had planted the drugs. That's when it all came out about James.'

'Revenge?' he suggested with a deep sigh. 'For rejecting her? For informing the school? For telling her she wasn't welcome in my home any more? For telling her to keep away from Natalia?'

'I suppose that makes sense,' she admitted heavily. 'She hates you as much as she hates him.'

Andreas inhaled. As much as he felt for the screwed-up Violet and the atrocious, immoral way she had been used by that monster, he couldn't rid himself of the anger that Carrie had thought of him in the same light, had been willing to think him corrupt and immoral too, had used her position as a journalist to get vengeance for something in which he was innocent.

'You know, it would have saved a lot of grief

if you had confronted me with Violet's allegations when she made them.'

'Truth or lie, you would have denied it,' she answered flatly. 'I wouldn't have trusted your answer.'

'Natalia would have confirmed it if you had asked.'

'Natalia hero-worshipped you. She would have said anything you told her to.'

'Are you saying you still don't believe me?' he asked with incredulity.

'I don't know what I believe.' Suddenly, she laughed, the sound startling, cutting through the heavy sadness that had brewed between them. But it contained no humour. 'You've led me on an un-merry dance for two days. I would have to be mad to trust you, of all people, and quite frankly I don't trust anyone, especially not rich, powerful men who are used to bending people to their will and stamping on anyone who gets in their way and think the laws of the land are for lesser mortals to obey. And you're one of the richest and most powerful of the lot.'

She turned her back on him and stepped over to the lawn, walking to the stone wall that separated his immaculate garden from the rocks and sand that led to his beach, and put her hands on it, tilting her face to look up at the stars. The moonlight cast her silhouette in an ethereal glow. Seeing her like that sent a strange ache through him.

He wanted to touch that effervescent skin. He wanted to grab those shoulders and shake the truth into her.

Her reached her in four long strides.

'You know damn well I speak the truth,' he said, standing behind her and placing a hand on her shoulder. 'I saw it in your eyes. Your sister lied to you about me. You know it and I know it.'

She went rigid under his touch. When she spoke, there was a breathless quality to her words. 'I'm a journalist. I deal with proof.'

'You lied to infiltrate my life,' he reminded her. 'Where was your proof then?'

'I infiltrated you in the hope of finding it but it doesn't matter any more, does it? You're safe. You rumbled me. Any dirt or skeletons in your closet will stay hidden. You'll get on with your life and I'll return to London and try to forget this whole mess ever happened. At least I can take comfort that I managed to get James put down for his crimes. Now take your hand off me.'

Although Carrie stood with her back to him, she was painfully aware of his stare burning into her just as his touch was doing.

He removed his hand as she asked but before she could exhale he leaned into her, his warm breath breezing through her hair as he spoke into her ear.

She squeezed her eyes shut and held her breath.

'Ah, *matia mou*, you think this is the end of it and I'm going to let you leave? Just like that?'

Closing her eyes was no barrier, she realised with silent desperation. The heat emanating from him seeped into her, the warmth of his breath playing through the strands of her hair and tickling her earlobes, sending tiny shivers dancing over her skin and into her bloodstream.

How could she *still* react like this to him? Whether or not he spoke the truth about his acquaintance with James and his role in Violet's expulsion—and if she believed that then she would have to believe Violet had lied to her—he'd played her like his own personal puppet.

She clenched her hands into fists and turned to look him in the eye. 'You said I couldn't leave here until I'd told you the truth. Well, you've had the truth and now I can go.'

He gave a sound that was like the antithesis of a laugh and stepped back but not far enough for her to dare move. He was still too close. She could still breathe in his scent and feel his warmth.

His eyes bore into hers, mesmerising her with the depth of their strength.

'I said you couldn't leave until I'd had the

truth, that is correct,' he mused thoughtfully, his voice as hypnotising as his stare. 'But I never said you would be leaving without me. I foiled your attempt to infiltrate my life and my business but now I have the staff of your paper, some of the most respected journalists in the world, thinking about me and wondering what kind of man I really am. There are already whispers in the media circulating about me. You have set something in motion, *matia mou*. Suspicions have been roused.'

Carrie's heart was beating so hard she had to fight to speak through its heavy echo in her throat. 'I will tell them I made a mistake.'

'Enough of the lies,' he whispered. 'You still think I am corrupt. Even if I believed you would say you had made a mistake and was able to say it convincingly, it wouldn't be enough. The doubts will linger. Every time a journalist sees my name the kernels of doubt will start again. My business will come under much closer scrutiny.'

'If you have nothing to hide then you have nothing to worry about.'

'If only it were that simple.' He grimaced and finally stepped away from her and walked back to the table.

Carrie rubbed her arms, the sudden removal of his warmth producing chills on her skin.

'All it takes is a few enquiring words in the wrong ears and the seeds of doubt are sown,' he said, picking up the whisky bottle. 'My clients invest their money with me because they trust me. They trust my ethics. It is a reputation I have cultivated with great care—it is the reason I refused James's business; I didn't trust him or his ethics. Once that trust is cast into doubt the repercussions can be disastrous, something I know from my parents' bitter experience. I am not prepared to take any risks with my business's health or with my reputation.'

He poured himself another drink, shaking his head with such faux regret that Carrie's internal danger signals fired back into red alert.

Raising his glass, he said, 'There is only one thing that will kill your colleagues' suspicions and the suspicions of anyone else who knows you've been investigating me. You will have to marry me.'

She stared at him, her brain freezing, her vocal cords stunned into silence.

He had to be playing more games…

'It is the only thing that will work,' he said with a decisive nod. 'You are a respected journalist. You have a reputation for fearlessness. You fight the underdog's corner. You fight for justice. If you marry me any lingering doubt about Samaras Fund Management will be killed stone dead.'

The idea of marrying her had first occurred to Andreas on the flight over, a plan he had sincerely hoped he would never have to enact. Embezzlement, though, was too serious an accusation to let slide. He had to nullify the rumours before they gained traction.

'It's the most stupid thing I've ever heard,' she whispered, her voice barely discernible in the breeze.

He took a drink and welcomed the spicy burn. 'Either you marry me or I send a copy of your confession to the proprietor of your newspaper, to my lawyer and to the police. I don't know how many laws you've broken but you've certainly broken all the ethics you're supposed to aspire to. Marry me or you're finished. Your career will be over, you might even go to prison.'

'What confession?' Her voice had strengthened. 'I haven't signed anything.'

With slow deliberation, he pulled his phone out of his top pocket where he'd put it since she discovered the hidden cameras.

'No,' she breathed.

'Yes.' He smiled grimly. 'I recorded every word.' To prove his point, he pressed play. Interference crackled loudly through the stillness of the night, then:

'You know, don't you?'

'That you're the undercover journalist Carrie Rivers?'

'You hateful bastard!' She stormed so quickly over to him she appeared to fly, until she was before him, her entire body trembling and her shaking hand held out to him. 'Give me that phone.'

'I think not.' He stopped the recording and tucked it back in his pocket. 'If you're thinking of stealing it from me, it's backed up automatically. But you're welcome to try.' He stood still and raised his hands in the air as if in supplication.

The look on her beautiful face could freeze lava. 'I can't believe you would be so underhand and deceitful.'

He lowered his hands and shrugged, unmoved. 'You're the journalist. Deceit is second nature to you as you have already proved. You were attempting to destroy me. I reserve the right to protect myself with whatever means I deem necessary. Under the circumstances, I would say I'm being generous. I am giving you the chance to save your career, your freedom and your privacy. And let us not forget your newspaper's fine reputation. Oh, and your sister.'

'Violet?' Her eyes widened alarmingly. 'You leave her out of this.'

'How can I when this is all about her? She is on the transcript. Everything we discussed is recorded. I don't imagine that everyone who hears it will be discreet—how long do you think before the tabloids get hold of it? Loose lips, *matia mou*…

'All you have to do is marry me for…let us say six months. Yes, that is a decent amount of time. Give me six months of marriage and then I will destroy the recording and all back-ups.'

'You can't expect me to give up six months of my life for you!'

He gazed at her pityingly. 'You should have thought of that before you began your vendetta against me. I am a good man. I am loyal to my family and my friends. I do not cheat in life or in love. But I am not a man to cross and you, *matia mou*, have crossed me and now you must accept the consequences.'

Her shoulders rose and then sagged as if in defeat, and she took the steps back to her seat and slumped onto it.

'Drink?' he asked, sliding into the seat next to hers and stretching his legs out.

She shook her head blankly before looking at him. 'You can't want to marry me.'

'I have no wish to marry at all, least of all to a poisonous viper like you.'

'Then *don't*.'

'I will do whatever is necessary to protect my business and my reputation.' He rolled his shoulders and looked at her. 'I've been waiting more than fifteen years for the freedom to do whatever the hell I want; I can wait another six months for it. And, you know, I think a marriage to you could be fun.'

'It will be hell. I'll make sure of it.'

He laughed. 'I'm sure you will, *matia mou*, but you *are* going to marry me. My cousin is marrying a week on Saturday. You will come as my guest and we will announce our engagement then.'

'What?'

Ignoring her outrage, he continued. 'We will marry by the end of the month. The sooner we do it, the sooner we can separate and get back to our real lives.'

'No one will believe it.' Hysteria crept into her voice. 'I don't want to marry, especially not a rich man, and everyone I work with knows that.'

'You have made your feelings about rich men very clear,' he said drily. 'One could accuse you of having a prejudice against us.'

'I *do*.'

'Then you will have to act to the very best of your ability to convince people that you've fallen in love and changed your mind, won't you?' He reached out a hand and fingered her hair.

She slapped it away. 'There is no way I can pretend to have fallen in love with you; I hate everything about you.'

'That is good because I hate everything about you too. Won't that make everything much more fun?'

'Fun?' she practically shrieked. 'You're mad!'

'Not mad,' he corrected. 'Practical. I could look at your beautiful face and allow myself to be furious with you for your vendetta against me and the potential it has to destroy everything I've spent a lifetime working for, or I can flip it around and enjoy the fact that the woman who would have done me such harm is locked to my side. You can behave exactly as you want behind closed doors but you can and will make the world believe you have fallen madly and passionately in love with me, because if anyone doubts it the deal is off and I expose your underhand, illegal dealings to the world and your sister's name will be dragged into it. Do it my way and we both keep our reputations and Violet gets to stay under whatever rock she is currently hiding under.'

She breathed deeply through her nose, the baleful glare she was casting him developing an air of resignation. 'How do I know I can trust you to destroy the recording?'

'It is a gamble you're going to have to take

but I *am* a man of my word and if you stick to your part of the arrangement I will stick to mine.' He cupped her cheek and brushed his fingers over the satin skin and felt the tiniest hitch of her breath before her hand rose to slap his away again. He caught it and pulled it to his chest.

'Don't pretend you don't welcome my touch, *matia mou*,' he murmured. 'We've finally been honest about everything else so why pretend? There is an attraction between us, a desire. You know it and I know it. We are going to live together for many months so why deny it?'

Her eyes held his for the longest time, a dozen emotions flickering through them, her lips pulled in tightly. Then they parted, the hazel eyes flashed and she tilted her head. 'You are suffering from what I like to call Rich Man's Delusion.'

He brought her hand to his lips and razed a kiss over her fingertips. 'Oh, yes? And what is that?'

'It's a syndrome only found in the ridiculously wealthy man.' Her voice had dropped, become breathy. Seductive. It whispered through his skin and seeped into his loins. 'It makes him think he's irresistible. I quite understand why a man like you would suffer from it—your wealth acts as a magnet to many women, I appreciate that, but sufferers, in their arrogance, then think *every* woman is attracted to him. It's beyond your concept that a woman can look at you and not want to drop her knickers.'

Rising from her seat, she gently removed her hand from his hold and palmed his cheek so she stood over him, the tip of her nose almost touching his.

Her pretty fingers caressed his cheek and, *Theos*, his skin revelled in the sensation, little sparks firing through the rest of him, heating him like a gently firing furnace.

She moved her hand to thread through his hair. 'I don't desire you,' she whispered, her lips so close to his that if he made a sudden movement they would fuse together, her sweet breath warm on him. 'I don't want you. If I did, I wouldn't be able to do this…'

The plump lips he'd stared at for hours imagining their feel and taste brushed against his in the whisper of a kiss.

For a moment Andreas did nothing but close his eyes and savour what might possibly be the most erotic moment of his life.

Her lips pressed a little more to his, still not fused, tentative but breathing him in, sweet yet sensuous, his loins, already charged, responding as his blood thickened and all his senses sprang to life.

Right at the moment he sensed her nerve failing her, he hooked an arm around her waist and jerked her to him. As he pulled her onto his lap she gave a tiny gasp and he took ruthless advantage of it, sweeping his tongue into her mouth and holding her tightly, primal lust surging through him. Her lips were softer than a pillow and moulded to his perfectly as he deepened the kiss, savouring her taste and the shape of her body pressed so compactly to his, the furnace heating his blood fired to a roar.

Her hands clasped at his skull, her fingers massaging into him, her mouth moving with his own as if they had fused into one entity.

She fitted perfectly into him, he thought dimly, sweeping a hand over her back and then round to stroke her stomach, which pulled in with a spasm at his touch, a moan so faint it could have been the breeze vibrating from her. He slid his hand up and rubbed his thumb on the underside of her breast, felt its softness through the fabric of her dress, but before he could touch any more she jolted and dragged her mouth from his.

Her fingers still clasping his skull, her breathing erratic, kiss-bruised lips parted, she gazed at him with confused heavy-lidded eyes before whipping her hands away and scrambling off his lap.

Looking anywhere but at him, she ran her hands through her hair and straightened her dress.

Andreas swallowed and took in air, the aching weight in his groin making it hard to think let alone speak. Only the heaviness of their breaths and the beats of his thundering heart cut through the stillness of the night.

When she looked at him again some semblance of composure had returned that would have fooled him if her voice didn't sound so breathy when she said, 'See? If I desired you I wouldn't be able to walk away from that.'

Then she turned and walked away from him to the French doors, her head high, her back magnificently straight. Only the tiny missteps she took showed she was as affected by what they had just shared as he.

'Next time, *matia mou*,' he called after her, his own voice hoarse, 'you will not be able to walk away.'

She didn't look back. 'There won't be a next time.'

'Do you want to put money on that?'

She didn't answer.

A moment later she had disappeared into his house.

MICHELLE SMART

Looking anywhere but at him, she ran her hands through her hair and straightened her clothes.

Andreas swallowed and took in the sobering weight in his gut, quashing it hard to drink her alone, savouring the closeness of their breaths and the beat of his thundering heart out through the stillness of the night.

CHAPTER SEVEN

CARRIE LAY FULLY dressed and wide awake under the covers of the narrow bed, kicking herself for not finding another room to sleep in, one far away from Andreas. If she weren't so afraid of bumping into him on the landing she would move to another room now. She didn't need to stay in this one any more. He was hardly going to fire her.

She laughed into her pillow, a maniacal sound that she immediately smothered.

If she'd heard that noise from anyone else she would assume they were mad.

Was she mad? Had all the glorious sun that had shone on her these past two days infected her mind and driven her out of it?

It was as good an explanation as anything, she supposed, to justify her behaviour.

Twenty minutes after crawling under the bedsheets and she still couldn't get her head around what had possessed her to play with fire like that.

She'd wanted to prove a point to him and wipe that smug grin off his face but it had gone too far. *She* had gone too far.

His touch…it had scorched her. She could still feel the imprint of his lips on hers and had to stop herself from rubbing her fingers over them. And she could still feel the contours of his body pressed against her. Her blood still felt fizzy, an ache in her loins she'd never known before.

Her brain burned just to remember it. It burned to remember the effort it had taken to walk away. They had been the hardest steps she'd ever taken, fighting her own yearning body.

Her first kiss.

She gritted her teeth and wished she were in a place where she could scream her frustration. She shouldn't be reliving their kiss, she should be trying to think of ways to get out of marrying him.

Marriage! To him!

And he was deadly serious about it too.

Violet was his trump card. If it were only Carrie's future at stake she would tell him to stuff it and take her chances. She'd been prepared to lose her job and her freedom before she'd embarked on investigating him, but that recording had changed everything. Andreas was too well known and her professional name too renown for that recording not to be dynamite to the tabloid press. Andreas would probably deliver a copy of it to them himself or upload it onto social media if she refused to go ahead with his plan, and then the whole world would hear him talk of how her sister had tried to seduce him and her affair with James and all those other awful things.

She screwed her eyes tight shut, fighting the fresh panic clawing at her chest.

That recording must never find its way into the public domain. Violet's recovery was too fragile and nebulous to cope with that. She didn't want her sister to have an excuse to dive back into the horrid, seedy world that had almost killed her.

A sliver of hazy light filtered the gap in the heavy curtains. Night was fading, the sun was rising and Andreas still hadn't come to bed.

Rubbing her hand over her forehead, she rolled over so her back was to the door.

What was the point in moving rooms? she thought as hot tears prickled her eyes. She would be sharing a roof with him for the next six months.

She was trapped.

Andreas stepped onto the veranda and breathed in the hot salty air, trying to clear the last of his lethargy away.

Going to bed after the sun had risen had not been conducive for a decent sleep but he'd thought it safer to wait until he could comfortably walk before putting himself an unlocked door's distance from Carrie.

He'd dreamed of her, hot lusty dreams as disturbing as they had been erotic, waking to the taste of her kisses on his tongue. He hardly ever remembered his dreams but these were still vivid, playing like a reel in his mind.

The real kisses they'd shared were still vivid in his mind too. He smiled to remember the little stumble she'd made when she'd walked away from him, her nonchalant charade not fooling either of them.

She wanted him. It had been there in the heat of her kisses and the heat from her flesh.

She really thought she could resist the attraction for the six months they would be married?

He'd known her for mere days but knew, as he knew his own name, that Carrie would resist until her stubborn little feet got sore.

It was more than mere stubbornness. When she set herself on a path it needed a bulldozer to steer her off it. Look at her work, the powerful men she had exposed, the focus and dedication it had taken to infiltrate their organisations and find the evidence needed to expose them.

And then there was her unflinching support

for her sister and her stubborn refusal to accept the truth about what had happened those years ago when she knew—and he was certain that deep down she did know—that he spoke the truth.

She'd believed him to be the friend of a monster, a thought that darkened his mood. Carrie had believed him capable of setting up a teenage girl with drugs. She believed him to be the same as the men she'd described who didn't think twice about stamping on lesser mortals if they got in their way.

There were many men in his circles who did behave like that, men who believed their wealth and position in society gave them free rein to do exactly as they pleased and generally they were right. Society turned a blind eye unless irrefutable evidence of the kind that tenacious journalists like Carrie produced meant action had to be taken.

She believed he was just like them. She believed he'd become seduced by the trappings of his wealth and lost his soul.

He inhaled even more deeply and closed his eyes, letting the burst of anger flow into his lungs and then expelling it out of his body.

His father had held onto his anger at the business rivals who had used such cruel tactics to destroy his business and it had put him in hospital with a failing heart. Deal with the root cause of the anger, punish those that needed it and move on—that was Andreas's way.

Carrie had held onto her hatred towards him for three years. She'd bided her time, taken out James first and then had decided the time was right to strike at him.

He took much satisfaction in knowing he'd cut her off at the head and foiled her plans. Marrying her ensured his business and reputation would be safe. And what were six months? As he'd told Carrie, he'd already waited fifteen years for his freedom so a few extra weeks were nothing.

At least those months would be eventful, something he'd not had the luxury of allowing his life to be since he'd left his Greek Island of Gaios for the adventure that was America. He'd planned out his whole life: work hard and play hard at university then work hard and play hard as he built a financial business for himself and then, and only after he'd enjoyed everything life had to offer, find someone to settle down with.

Of those three goals only the first had been achieved and he looked back on his university days with nostalgia.

No sooner had he graduated than he'd discovered the dire mess his parents were in.

Movement behind him made him turn. A member of his staff had brought him a tray of food, a light mezze to sustain him, the time being closer to lunch than breakfast and the sun already burning hot.

'Have you seen Carrie?' he asked. He'd knocked on her door before leaving his bedroom and, when there had been no answer, had taken a quick look and found her room empty, her bed neatly made.

A shake of the head. 'Do you want me to look for her?'

'Don't worry about it. Let me know when she turns up.'

She couldn't have gone far, he assured himself. He kept just one car here, in an outhouse and for emergency purposes only, and there was only one road off the peninsular. It would be impossible to take his car or his speedboat without someone seeing or hearing.

Pouring his coffee first, he was helping himself to melon and yogurt when he caught a glimpse of a figure walking along the beach in his direction.

The tightness he hadn't noticed in his chest loosened.

He watched her while he ate as, step by step, she came into clearer focus, the memory of their kiss playing in his mind all over again.

'Good morning, *matia mou*,' he said when she reached the table. 'Have you eaten?'

She shook her head, her eyes hidden behind the designer shades he'd bought her. They were the only things he could see that she was wearing that he'd provided her with. Today, in temperatures already in the high-twenties and guaranteed to rise much higher, Carrie wore the outfit he'd interviewed her in, her cashmere jumper and grey trousers, which she'd rolled up to lay mid-calf. Her feet were bare.

'Coffee?' he asked, reaching for the pot.

There was a tiny hesitation before she nodded and sat down in the seat furthest from him. 'I didn't think you knew how to pour coffee.'

'Now that my minion has been upgraded to fiancée I thought I should reacquaint myself with the simple tasks I have always done for myself. And for the record, I have never expected a proper employee to perform the slavish chores I got you to do. I'm no man-child.'

He poured the coffee, added a splash of milk and one spoonful of sugar, and pushed the cup over to her.

'Thank you.' A tiny smile played on her lips. 'I didn't realise you'd paid attention to how I take my coffee.'

'I pay attention to everything, *matia mou*, especially with you.'

She tilted her head to look up at the sky then gathered her hair together and tied it into a knot without using any kind of device to hold it in place.

'Feeling hot, are you?' he asked drily. 'Maybe you should consider changing into clothing more suited to the weather.'

She took her cup and cradled it in both hands. 'Now I'm no longer your minion I can wear what I like, and what I like to wear are clothes that don't expose all my flesh.'

'Afraid you will drive me wild with desire?'

'You're putting words in my mouth,' she said stiffly.

'I have managed to keep my hands to myself since we arrived here and you have had plenty of flesh on display.' As he spoke he helped himself to a fresh bread roll and cut into it. A delicious yeasty aroma was released, a smell almost as good as Carrie's scent, and he inhaled it greedily. 'After all, you were the one to kiss *me, matia mou.* Do you need to cloak yourself to resist me?'

The knuckles holding her cup had turned white. 'I kissed you to prove a point. It meant nothing to me.'

'And you proved it very well. If I'd had any doubt that you desire me, your kiss dispelled it.'

'The fact I walked away proves I felt nothing.'

Digging his knife into a pot, he slathered jam over his roll. 'It proves that you have mastered the art of walking. For the avoidance of doubt, I am prepared to be used by you whenever you want to prove that you don't desire me. Any time at all. Day or night.' Then he bit into his roll.

Carrie fought hands that wanted to shake and put the cup to her mouth to drink her coffee, closing her mind to the vivid images playing in her mind of being in his arms and the hunger of his mouth on hers.

After three hours of sleep she'd woken from dreams already fading into haziness but which her body ached to recapture. Then everything that had passed between them had come back to her in one huge rush, all the words, their kiss...

She'd jumped out of bed, dug her own clothes, which had been laundered by Andreas's staff, out of the wardrobe and put them on as a form of armour. Then she had escaped to walk on the beach, desperate to exercise the ache deep inside out of her system and clear her mind. It had all been pointless. She could cover herself from head to toe in sackcloth and she would still feel naked before him. She could walk a thousand miles and her stomach would still flip over when she looked into those piercing light brown eyes.

And he seemed to know it.

Putting the cup back on the table, she strove to compose herself, a difficult task when she felt as if she were sitting in a sauna, the heat from the sun and her body's reaction to merely sitting and talking to Andreas combining together to be almost unendurable. But endure she would. He had the upper hand over her life now but she wouldn't allow him to have the upper hand over her emotions and feelings too. 'I don't need to prove anything to you.'

He swallowed his food. 'You have six months to convince yourself of that. For now, you should eat something. We will be leaving soon.'

'Where are we going?'

'Back to London.'

Thank God for that.

It would get better when they were back there, she assured herself, when cold drizzle and concrete greeted her rather than brilliant blue skies and palm trees.

London was her home. Her territory. It was where she belonged.

She hid her relief to ask, 'What happened to your holiday?'

'We have wheels to set in motion, *matia mou*…a wedding to prepare.'

'You said we wouldn't announce our engagement until your cousin's wedding.'

'We still need to arrange our own and you need to return to work and inform your colleagues that the tip-off you had been given about me is completely unfounded and that you are so convinced of my innocence that you have fallen madly in love with me.'

She scoffed.

He laughed loudly. 'I'm sure faking mad, passionate love will not be a problem for such an accomplished actress as yourself.' Getting to his feet, he stretched his back. 'I'm going to have a swim in the pool before we leave. Can I tempt you to strip off those clothes that are making you so uncomfortable to join me?'

'I can't think of anything less tempting.'

He shrugged and whipped off his T-shirt, the movement sending a wave of his cologne into her senses. The sun shone down on his bare torso, his toned and oh-so-masculine physique seeming to shimmer under it.

Tiny pulses set off low inside her as she remembered just how good it had felt to be held so tightly against that body...

Moisture filled her mouth and she fisted her hands against her thighs while striving to keep her features neutral, fighting the fresh hunger uncoiling itself inside her.

For a long moment he stared at her. A smile played on the lips that had kissed her so thoroughly, before he placed his T-shirt on the back of his chair. 'Are you sure you're not tempted?'

'Very sure.' But she wished her voice sounded more convincing and that she was the only one to have heard the husky rasp that had come into it.

His eyes gleaming, he hunched over to whisper into her ear, 'Your mouth says one thing, *matia mou*, but your eyes say another. I know which I believe.'

The sensation of his warm breath against her skin was all too fleeting for no sooner had he spoken than he was striding away from her.

'You've only just eaten so try not to get a stitch while you're swimming,' she called out, forcing strength into her voice. 'It would be dreadful if you were to drown before we marry.'

He turned but didn't stop walking, surefooted even as he trod backwards. 'But it would mean you having to give me the kiss of life so it would be an excellent way to meet my maker.'

Then he winked and hardly broke stride to turn around again.

Carrie put a hand to her chest, her heart thumping hard against it, watching the long, muscular legs walk away from her.

Once he was out of sight, she took some deep breaths and closed her eyes.

It would all feel different when she was back on home soil.

It had to.

CHAPTER EIGHT

THE ELEGANT FIGURE stepped out of the revolving doors with an older woman a pace behind her, the two women chatting between themselves.

The older woman was the first to spot him standing against a black Bentley watching them. She nudged Carrie and nodded in his direction.

He raised a hand in greeting.

Carrie's eyes found his. Even with the distance separating them Andreas could see the high colour slashing her cheeks as she mimicked his greeting, then used the same hand to smooth a loose strand of hair that had fallen from the knot it had been tied into off her face, then to smooth her long cream overcoat. Her movements were rapid but her colleague noticed, a smile spreading on her face as she watched Carrie subconsciously groom herself.

After a beat, Carrie said something to her colleague, then walked steadily to him, chin aloft, her right hand clutching the strap of her handbag to her chest.

'This is a pleasant surprise,' she said when she reached him, speaking in a voice loud enough that those of her nearby colleagues, all hurrying to the nearby underground station in their eagerness to get home, would be able to hear. The inflection of surprise she put in it was a masterstroke.

Andreas had been waiting by his car for twenty minutes. He estimated a dozen of the people who had come out of the building that housed the *Daily Times* had done a double take at his presence outside their offices.

He gave a slow smile, feasting his eyes on the face that had consumed his thoughts all day. The wind picked up the strand of hair she'd only just smoothed down and he reached out to tuck it behind her delicate ear.

Her already coloured cheeks went a few shades darker, and her throat moved.

'I have been thinking of you all day,' he murmured for her ears only, delighting at the way her eyes pulsed at his words.

He'd dreamed about her again. She'd been the first thing on his mind when his eyes had opened that morning. By lunchtime he'd taken to checking his watch every few minutes, the time ticking down until their prearranged meet-

ing outside her work offices slowing to a le-
thargic snail's pace. He assured himself this
restlessness, this yearning to see her again was
due to his impatience to get the ball rolling in
the fake relationship they were about to establish. He desired Carrie but more than anything
his desire was to protect his business from the
lies she had told her zealous colleagues about
him.

In a clearer tone that anyone passing would
hear he added, 'I know it must sound crazy but
I was hoping you would let me take you out for
dinner.'

She swallowed, her eyes pulsing again before
she blinked it away. 'That sounds totally crazy
but…that would be lovely.'

'Excellent. Can I give you a lift home?'

'If it's not out of your way.'

'I wouldn't care if it was.' He grinned then
opened the back door for her and followed her
in.

The moment the door closed them in, her demeanour changed. Carrie perched herself rig-
idly beside him, knees tucked tightly together,
hands clasped on her lap.

Once they were moving in the heavy London
traffic, she said in a clipped voice, 'That must
have been difficult for you, having to ask po-
litely rather than just bark orders at me.'

'It was a nightmare. I'm used to people asking how high when I tell them to jump,' he replied drolly. 'How did it go today?'

She rested her head back on the leather seat and closed her eyes. 'We had a meeting about you. I said my tip-off had been wrong and that the person who gave it to me is refusing to answer my calls.'

'And that sounds plausible?'

'I've made it sound like my source is avoiding me. I'll give it a few days and say I met up with him and that he confessed he'd made it up for money.'

'And does *that* sound plausible?' He watched her response closely, looking for signs of an untruth or the bending of facts.

'It's not uncommon. We do pay for tips that are verified and lead to a story being printed, but it doesn't happen much. Most of the people who give us tip-offs do it because it's the right thing to do—we're not a tabloid, we deal with weighty stories that are often in the national interest.'

'Will they want to check with your source?'

'Our sources are sacrosanct. We never reveal them without the source's permission, not even to each other.'

Carrie rolled her shoulders, trying to ease the tension in them. Her colleagues had seemingly taken her story at face value—Andreas's instincts had been proven right in that regard—but the cramped feeling of guilt had spread its way inside her and through to her muscles.

It nauseated her to think of all the barefaced lies she had told her colleagues in recent weeks. When she'd embarked on the single-minded task of bringing Andreas down, she'd been so certain of his guilt and so filled with anger at what he'd done to her sister that she had smothered her own screaming conscience. Now she was lying to her supportive colleagues for a second time but what else could she do? If she didn't go ahead with Andreas's plan then her sister's name would be dragged into the world's consciousness and whatever recovery she'd made would be destroyed. Violet would be back on the drugs quicker than a wannabe vegetarian lion passing by a wounded gazelle; unable to resist.

'How did you explain my learning your true identity?' Andreas asked.

She could happily scream. She'd had almost a whole day away from him but he'd been breaking into her thoughts the whole time. She might as well have taken him to work with her. Her morning had been devoted to talking about him in the staff meeting, her afternoon fielding female colleagues' whispered questions about what he was *really* like, if he was as handsome in the flesh as in pictures...

Every time she'd been asked her cheeks had flushed. It had been excruciating. Half the office thought she had a crush on him without her having to say a word.

Andreas would be delighted if she told him, which of course she would not.

Instead, she told him in as cool a voice as she could muster—anything to counteract the skipping warmth being back with him was inducing, 'I said your PA had learned my references didn't check out after all—at least that wasn't a lie—and that by the time this was discovered, I was already convinced of your innocence. Exactly as we agreed.'

She felt him relax beside her, pressing his own head back against the seat and facing her. She kept her eyes facing forward, not looking at him.

He inched his face a little closer to her. 'You didn't like lying to your colleagues, did you?'

How could he read her so damn *well*? He barely knew her.

Her throat caught. 'I hate it,' she muttered. 'Lying on an investigation is never real because I always know I'm getting the facts needed to expose corrupt and illegal practices. This is very different.' She turned her head to meet his gaze. 'You know I'm only going along with this to protect Violet, don't you? If it was just my own future at stake I would let you throw me to the wolves.'

He brushed his thumb over her cheekbone lazily but there was an intensity in his stare. 'She is lucky to inspire such devotion.'

Carrie grabbed his hand, intending to push it off her face but instead wrapped her fingers around it tightly and stared back with matching concentration to his. 'Do we have to do this... this marriage thing?' she asked on impulse. 'My colleagues all believe I made a mistake. I've convinced them there's nothing worth investigating about you.'

His light brown eyes continued to ring into hers for a long time before he answered. There was none of the usual staccato beat to his voice, his tone slow and thoughtful. 'A good reputation takes years to build but can be knocked down in minutes by nothing more than careless words. Do you know what happened to my parents' business?'

She shook her head.

'They owned their own water taxi company. Do you know what that is?'

'Like a regular taxi firm but on water?'

He nodded. His face had inched so close to hers she could feel his warm breath on her skin.

A voice in her head warned her to shift away from him, not allow him to get any closer.

Carefully she released her hold on his hand but his eyes…

This was why she tried to avoid looking into them.

It was as if he were hypnotising her.

'They took tourists and locals island hopping or from one side of the island to another. They also had a handful of larger boats they chartered out for daytrips through the holiday companies. It was a good living for them.' His lips tightened, the mesmerising eyes darkening. 'When I was in my final year at university a rival company set itself up. These rivals were predators. They sabotaged my parents' fleet. One of the charter boats sank; it's a miracle none of the passengers were killed. Then rumours were spread that they knowingly employed paedophiles—can you imagine the impact that had on an island built for families? People stopped using their taxis, the holiday companies cancelled their contracts…in months the business they had spent their whole marriage building was in ruins.'

Chills raced up Carrie's spine. 'That's…horrific. What did your parents do?'

He grimaced and rolled his face away from hers. 'They tried to fight but did not have the resources. They had used all their savings to get me through university. I went on a scholarship but they paid for all my accommodation, flights back home for holidays… I thought they could afford it. If I had known they were putting themselves in such a precarious financial situation I would have worked more hours to support myself…' He cut himself off and shook his head before straightening in his seat.

His gaze fixed on the screen separating them from his driver, he continued, 'It is done. I cannot change what they did or what I did. I didn't go home at all in that last year. There was too much going on in my life. Studying. Girls. Parties. Too busy to call home and only listening with one ear when we did speak. I didn't have a clue what was happening with them. They didn't want to worry me and made my sister promise not to tell me. I learned the truth when I graduated.'

'Would you have been able to do anything if you had known?'

His jaw clenched before he answered. 'If they had told me when it first started I might have been able to scare their rivals off. I could have at least shared the burden with them. Once I did know, I helped as much as I could. Their financial situation was an incentive for me to work all hours so I could support them through it and pay for lawyers who were able to take the case to court. To prove the allegations wrong and prove that their rivals deliberately sabotaged their business. It took four years to get there but they went to prison for it.'

'Good,' she stated vehemently.

He turned his face to look at her. A faint smile appeared on his lips. 'I should have guessed that what happened to my parents would make you angry. You are a one-woman crusader against injustice.'

'I'm surprised I didn't already know about it.' She swallowed before giving a small, apologetic smile. 'I did a *lot* of research on you.'

His low laugh showed his lack of surprise at her confession. 'The press coverage was minimal and all in Greek. My name wouldn't have been in any of the reports—it all happened before I became well known.'

'How are your parents now?'

'In a good place, thank God, but it took them a long time to recover. The whole thing did not just affect their finances but everything else too. Their reputations and health were ruined. Friends, neighbours, people who knew them well, all shunned them. By the time it went to court what mattered most to them was having their reputations restored. It was a bitter thing for them to accept, that people believed them capable of knowingly employing child abusers. My mother has since fought two different forms of cancer and my father has had a quadruple heart bypass. Losing Tanya almost finished them off.'

'I'm sorry.' Her heart twisted for this couple she had never met who had been through so much pain and heartache.

And Andreas had lost his sister.

Carrie knew what the pain of loss felt like. Her mother had been dead for seven years now but there were still times when grief caught her; a song playing on the radio, seeing her shampoo on a supermarket shelf, little things that could poleaxe her.

She felt her heart wrench to imagine all the little things that could poleaxe Andreas with grief too.

When he reached for her hand and brought it to his lips she didn't snatch it away.

'It does not take a lot to destroy a reputation and a business,' he said sombrely as he brushed his lips over her fingertips. 'I will not take the risk of assuming the damage can be prevented with some carefully chosen words. Even a *whisper* of embezzlement could cause irreparable harm to my name and then who can say what the repercussions would be? Marrying you, the woman who started the whispers, is the best way to kill it.'

Her hand tingled, her fingers itching to open up and explore his face and touch all the hard, masculine features her eyes could not help but drink in…

'We are here.'

Blood roared so hard in her ears his softly delivered words sounded distant. 'What?'

'Your home. We have arrived. Are you going to invite me in?'

Coming to her senses with a jolt, Carrie snatched her hand from his and jerked back, then fumbled with the door handle, her sudden desperation for air that wasn't filled with his scent making her all fingers and thumbs. Before she could break the handle off, the driver appeared and opened it for her.

She practically threw herself out of the car. The cold drizzle was a welcome relief on her flushed skin.

'Carrie?'

She dragged the fresh air into her lungs before looking back at him. 'Yes?'

His eyes were alive with amusement, as if he knew exactly what had got her so flustered.

He probably did know. He seemed to be able to read her like a book.

'Tomorrow, we book our wedding.'

She shrugged, pretending a nonchalance she absolutely did not feel.

'And you need to book leave from your work.'

'I can hardly marry you if I'm in the office.'

He grinned. 'I meant for my cousin's wedding. It's being held in Agon, an island near Crete. We'll fly over at the weekend.'

'But the wedding's not for a fortnight.'

'We can spend the week before it there. I'm already bored of the English rain.'

'I can't just take a week off at this short notice.' She'd thought they would spend the weeks leading up to their marriage in London, in her home territory, where she was safe…

She hadn't been safe in the back of his car.

The cold English drizzle had proved no barrier to her ever-growing awareness of him.

'Tell them I've agreed to an exclusive interview with you.' His lively eyes carried steel in them, clearly saying, *You will do exactly as you are told or our deal is off.*

He had her exactly where he wanted her and he knew it.

'Fine. But you'll have to actually give me an exclusive interview in exchange.'

Now his eyes gleamed with more than mere amusement. 'There are many exclusive things I can give you, *matia mou*. An interview is just one of them.'

The gleam deepened, his suggestive words hanging in the air between them for what felt like a whole epoch before she got her vocal cords to work, her cheeks flaming like a bonfire. 'I'll book the time off.'

A knowing smile played on his lips. 'I will pick you up in two hours.'

'What for?'

'I am taking you out to dinner, *matia mou*.' The smile turned into the wickedest of grins. 'Unless you wish to invite me into your home and cook for me?'

'Hell will freeze over before I lift a finger for you again.'

He gave an ironic shake of his head at her defensiveness. 'It is funny how your mouth tells me one thing but your eyes and body the other.'

It was with great delight that she slammed the car door in his face.

When her front door was closed and locked for good measure she stood with her back against it, trying to breathe properly.

Being on home soil hadn't changed a thing.

The knock on the front door Carrie had been anticipating for the past ten minutes still made her jump and set her already skittish heart thrumming maniacally.

She took one last look in the mirror and

smoothed her hair, then breathed deeply as she walked down the stairs. Her shoes were ready by the front door and she slid her feet into them and removed her coat from the hook before she opened it.

After a mere five days in London it was time to get her passport out again.

Andreas stood at the threshold, dressed in a sharp navy suit with an open-necked white shirt, that wicked, wolfish grin on his face. 'Good morning, *matia mou*. You look as beautiful as ever.'

She rolled her eyes. 'Cut the cheesy lines, there's no one to hear you.'

Over the past five days they'd been on four 'dates', all in restaurants where the paparazzi liked to camp out. As he was a man who had always kept his private life discreet, the paparazzi responded to Andreas's presence as if he were Father Christmas bearing early gifts.

The lengths she had gone to in the past to keep her face hidden from public view, like all journalists who worked undercover, had been for nothing. That the Greek billionaire Andreas Samaras was dating the respected journalist Carrie Rivers had generated more excitement than even she had expected.

Her name would be linked to his for ever.

'It cannot be a line when it is the truth.' The

pulse in his eyes shot straight through her flesh and into her bloodstream. 'You *are* beautiful.'

Heat rose inside her, a now familiar throbbing ache.

When they dined out together he would stare at her with that same look, his eyes holding hers as he probed her with questions about her job and her interests, drawing her into conversation as any other dating couple behaved.

She'd been surprised at how...*easy* it had all been. She'd expected there to be awkwardness between them but Andreas had carried all the conversations with an easy-going wit, always keeping talk in safe territory, displaying a droll humour that often made her laugh without her having to fake it for the paparazzi lenses.

There had been moments when she had forgotten why they were there, forgotten that she hated him. Forgotten *why* she hated him; struggled to reconcile him with the man she'd spent three years dreaming of destroying.

And underlying everything lay the strange chemical cocktail that snaked between them. Always she refused to drink wine with their meals; his intoxicating presence enough for her to fight against without adding alcohol to the mix. She had to keep her defences up as much as she could, not blithely allow herself to lower them.

'Are you packed?' he asked.

She blinked sharply to clear her head—it seemed she was always having to clear it when with him—and nodded. 'My case is in the kitchen. Give me a…'

'I'll get it for you,' he interrupted with a wink, then swept past her and into the house. 'I have some papers for you to read through before we leave.'

Carrie couldn't help the laugh that burst out of her.

Until that moment, she had continued to refuse him admittance into her home. This was her territory, her sanctuary away from him, the one place she felt safe from all the turbulence that her life had become and the wild emotions he continually evoked in her.

She sighed and rolled her eyes. She had only been delaying the inevitable and, frankly, she was surprised she'd been able to keep him out of her home for this long. Andreas had proved himself to be a steamroller when it came to getting what he wanted done. Even at the registry office the other day when they'd gone to book their wedding, the date he'd wanted had been fully booked and yet somehow the registrar had been able to accommodate him for that particular date and for the exact time he wanted.

Carrie followed him down the long hallway behind the trail of his tangy cologne.

Breathing in his scent drove away her momentary amusement and replaced it with the tell-tale flutters of panic and with it a certainty that she would never be able to walk down this hallway again without thinking of him...

How could she know that?

Stop being so melodramatic, she chided herself grimly.

'This is nice,' he commented as he stepped into the airy high-ceilinged kitchen. 'It's much bigger than it looks from the outside.'

'Yes, it's a regular Tardis.'

'It's a good location too. It must have cost a lot of money to buy.'

'I guess so. It costs a fortune to maintain and heat.' The front looked out over Hyde Park but as a child the monetary value of such a prime location had meant nothing to her. She remembered sunny days there, going for picnics, curling up on her mother's lap under a tree as she read her stories, remembered teaching Violet how to do cartwheels and walk on her hands. Remembered dropping her ice cream and trying so hard to be grown up and not cry about it and Violet, chubby legged and her hair in pigtails, toddling over to her.

'You eat mine too, Cawwie...'

She blinked the bittersweet memories away before they could lance her heart any more.

She'd spoken to Violet only the day before, another stilted conversation but this time it had been stilted on both sides, the question Carrie most wanted to ask she'd found herself incapable of saying: *Did you lie about Andreas setting you up?*

She hadn't asked because she was afraid of the answer. She was afraid that even if Violet's answer was negative, she might not believe it.

'I've lived here since I was four,' she explained, speaking over the fresh roil of nausea that was induced whenever she allowed those doubts to gain too much space in her head. 'My stepdad bought it when he married my mum. She got it when they divorced.' And Carrie and Violet had inherited it when she'd later died. 'What were the papers you wanted me to look at?'

He pulled a thick envelope out of his inside pocket and held it out. 'It's a draft of our pre-nuptial agreement.'

'What pre—?' She caught herself and shook her head. 'Of course. You're protecting yourself.'

'Anyone in my position would protect himself but you will see I have made more than adequate provisions for you.'

'Unless that document says we both walk away with nothing from each other I don't want to read it. I don't want your money.'

Andreas stared at her beautiful set face.

Had there ever been a more stubborn person in the history of the earth?

He thought of the thousands of pounds' worth of designer goods she'd left behind in the Seychelles, giving them to one of Sheryl's young daughters who was the same dress size. He only knew this because an anxious Sheryl had called him to make sure it was okay for her daughter to have them.

That Carrie had done this shouldn't have surprised him when he considered she'd spent their last day there sweltering in her own clothes rather than changing into any of the items he'd bought for her. It had still stung though, just as her refusal to take the envelope from his hand and read it also stung. She would much rather overheat than wear something paid for by him. She would rather struggle to pay her heating bill than accept a cash sum from him that would keep her comfortable for life.

If she were starving she would still refuse his money.

And he'd thought they'd been making progress.

She still believed him to be corrupt.

'Carrie,' he said, making sure to keep his tone moderate although he wanted to snarl his words at her, 'I'm only giving you what a court would award you on our divorce.'

'I don't want it. I earn my own money.'

He shook his head, incredulity and anger merging like a toxin inside him. 'You are unbelievable.'

'Why? Because I won't play the money roulette game? I'm only marrying you to protect my sister. I don't want your money. The only thing you could give me that I would want is a time machine that can fast forward the next six months.'

He held the envelope up. 'You are sure about this? You are certain you want to give up a small fortune?'

'Yes,' she answered without any hesitation.

'I'll get a new one done, then, that spells out you receive *nothing*.' He ripped the envelope in half and let the pieces fall to the floor. Then he stepped over them to the large old-fashioned suitcase by the kitchen table. 'And now that that is settled, we can go. Maybe some sunshine will make you more agreeable although I doubt anything could.'

CHAPTER NINE

CARRIE OPENED THE French doors of the living room of the lavish Mykonian-style villa she had been given for her stay on Agon and looked out over its beautiful garden. Fruit trees had come into blossom, filling the air with the most wonderful spring scent. She breathed it in deeply, letting it calm her ragged nerves.

The island itself was dazzling, mountainous and overlooked by blue skies, but that was where the similarity with the Seychelles ended. Andreas's peninsular had been remote, his and the chef's cottage the only homes for miles and miles. Agon was filled with pristine white homes, its beaches golden where the Seychelles sand was white. There was a different feel to it too, different smells and a much different vibe. This was a rich island and a growing financial powerhouse. Carrie's villa would befit royalty and if she were in a different frame of mind she would be delighting to find herself staying in such a beautiful place for the next week.

She didn't know if the villa was hers alone or if Andreas was sharing it with her. She hadn't seen him since his driver had dropped her off and brought their cases in while Andreas waited in the car. His only words as she'd got out of the vehicle had been, 'I'll be back by seven to take you out for dinner.'

Since they had left her London home that morning he had hardly exchanged three sentences with her. His cases were still by the front door. If he were planning to stay here they would have been taken to whichever of the six bedrooms had been appointed as his.

A housekeeper and a general handyman had been in the villa to greet her and show her to her room, the handyman carrying her case up the marble stairs for her.

Her bedroom had taken her breath away; it was the complete opposite of the box room she'd been given in the Seychelles. She'd then been given a tour of the rest of the place and given the phone number for the staff house, where a small army of workers lived, all available twenty-four-seven for whatever she needed.

She'd been alone now for three hours and time was dragging insufferably. She'd had a bath in her en-suite bathroom, feeling decadent in the freestanding roll-top bath, and then had changed into a pretty summer top in a light peach colour with spaghetti straps and a full matching skirt that fell to mid-calf. The top half of it especially was very similar to the summer dresses Andreas had bought for her but…this didn't feel as good. The clothing he'd bought for her had caressed her skin in a way she hadn't realised until she'd put her own, much cheaper clothing back on.

She'd paced from room to room ever since, checking her watch every few minutes.

She checked it again and bit her lip.

It was almost seven.

Nerves were accumulating in her belly at an ever-increasing rate, far more violent nerves than she'd become used to when waiting for him to pick her up for their dates in London.

She'd angered him and while it was a thought that should make her glad, it made her stomach feel all coiled and acid-filled. In all that had passed between them in the past week she'd forgotten what it felt like to be on the receiving end of his anger, as she had been three years ago when he'd lasered her with his stare outside the headmistress's office.

He'd been angry the night when the truth had been revealed between them but that had felt different. They'd both been angry—furious—

with each other. Since then he'd been all charm and geniality and she didn't think it was an act. He was that way with everyone, treated even underpaid and always undervalued waiting staff in restaurants as if their opinions on the dish of the day truly mattered, made a point of learning their names and *remembering* them.

She couldn't help thinking that her refusal to open his envelope had wounded him in some way, which she knew was a ridiculous notion...

Footsteps treading on the marble floor sounded out behind her and she spun round to find him standing there holding an enormous bunch of red roses.

Their eyes met and held, and her heart made the most enormous thud against her ribs, the motion knocking all the air from her lungs.

There was no humour in his eyes, no knowing gleam, not even any anger, just a steadfast openness that made the thuds in her heart morph into a racing thrum.

He'd changed into fresh clothes, tailored dark grey trousers and a black shirt, since he'd dropped her at the villa. But there was something unkempt about him, his hair a little messier than he usually wore it, his jaw thick with stubble when he'd always been freshly shaved on their dates.

He held the flowers out to her. 'Peace offering.'

She paused for only a moment before taking them from him.

'Thank you,' she whispered.

She'd never been given flowers before.

Keeping her eyes on his, she rubbed her nose against the delicate petals. They smelt wonderful.

'You look beautiful,' he said simply.

Her heart now racing so hard she could imagine it bursting out of her ribs, she attempted a smile but found one impossible to form.

'I'll find a vase to put these in.' Forcing her feet to uproot themselves from the floor, she walked past him and headed to the vast kitchen on the other side of the villa.

Andreas kept step beside her. 'Have you settled in all right?'

'Yes, thank you.' She hadn't found it this awkward to talk to him since the interview in his office. Back then, her tongue had been tied with the fear of being discovered. Her fear now was of a completely different hue. 'Have you had a good afternoon?'

'It has been productive.'

'Oh?' They'd reached the vast kitchen.

Carrie put the flowers on a worktop and immediately busied herself opening cupboards and drawers, ostensibly to find a vase but more to keep her attention diverted from him and the terrifying things happening inside her.

'I had a meeting.' He opened a high cupboard and took down a crystal vase. 'Is this what you're looking for?'

She took it from him with a small smile of thanks and almost dropped it when their fingers brushed.

A shock of electricity skipped over her skin and danced into her veins, and she hurriedly turned her back to him as she muttered her thanks.

Just breathe.

First she filled the vase with water and added the sachet of feed to it.

Breathe.

She'd spotted scissors earlier when she'd made herself coffee, and she grabbed them out of the drawer and cut the pretty cellophane wrapping around the roses, then took the first rose—thankfully the thorns had been removed—and cut an inch of the base off and put it in the vase. She grabbed another, certain she remembered her mother doing something else when she was given roses but her brain was overloaded, trying to focus on the task at hand while tuning out the huge figure standing so close to her.

She could feel his eyes on her.

As she reached for another rose, a warm

hand pressed into her lower back while another wrapped around her reaching wrist.

She couldn't move. She couldn't breathe. Her blood had thickened to a sludge that pulsed through every crevice in her body.

Andreas felt the pulse in Carrie's wrist beat madly against his thumb, the only movement on her still frame.

Theos, he wanted her so badly it had become a constant ache he carried everywhere with him.

He'd been so damned *angry* with her and her stubborn refusal to take her blinkers off when it came to him.

When he'd dropped her at the villa he'd had half a mind to check himself into a hotel for the night but then he'd left his meeting hours later and a woman in a soft-top convertible had driven past him, roof down. She'd had chestnut hair almost identical in colour to Carrie's. His chest had contracted so tightly in that moment he'd had to fight for breath.

Why should he care what Carrie thought of him? he'd told himself as he'd dragged air into his lungs. She was only going to be in his life for a short period. All that mattered was that she marry him and kill the rumours before they properly started.

But even as he was thinking all that he'd

found himself walking into a florist and asking for their largest bunch of roses.

He'd never bought flowers for a woman before.

It had been the look in Carrie's eyes as he'd passed the flowers to her that had driven the last of his anger out. There had been a vulnerability in those eyes he'd never seen in her before.

He leaned forward to breathe in her cloud of hair, the silky strands tickling his nose, and heard a jagged inhalation.

His need for her, the compulsion to touch her, the yearn to taste her... He had never wanted a woman more.

He breathed the fragrant scent of her hair in again then cupped her cheeks in his hands, his body almost touching hers, close enough to feel the tiny quivers vibrating through her.

Stark, frozen hazel eyes stared into his, her trembling lips parted but no sound coming out.

'I'm going to kiss you,' he said huskily. 'I'm going to kiss you until you tell me to stop.' Then, caressing her cheeks with his fingers, he pressed his lips to hers...

At first she remained stock still, not even breathing, her body like soft concrete. Slipping his hands round to spear her hair and cradle her head in much the same way she had cradled his what now felt like a lifetime ago, he moulded his mouth a little more firmly to hers, gently coaxing her into a response he knew she was fighting with everything she had.

Stubbornly, she continued to resist, her body still rigid, her soft plump lips refusing to move with his. But she didn't push him away or tell him to stop.

Emboldened, he gently moved his mouth over hers and ran a hand down the length of her back.

He felt her give the tiniest of shivers.

Then she took the tiniest of breaths.

And she still didn't push him away or tell him to stop.

He pressed himself a little closer, trapping her against the worktop.

She gasped into his mouth then quickly closed her own again but made no effort to break away from his kiss.

And still she didn't push him away or tell him to stop.

His mouth still covering hers, Andreas brushed his hands lightly down her sides and clasped her hips, then in one movement broke the kiss to lift her onto the worktop. Her hands sprang to life and grabbed his arms as if to steady herself.

Her eyes fluttered open.

For a moment that passed like an age, they stared into each other's eyes, Carrie's hooded gaze pulsing dazed desire at him. The hands holding his biceps like a vice loosened but she didn't let go.

Suddenly desperate to feel the softness of her lips against his again, he crushed his mouth to hers and gently pushed her thighs apart through the fabric of her skirt and stepped into the space he'd just created so the unmistakable feel of his arousal pressed against her pelvis, obvious even with all the layers of thin clothing separating them.

Her breaths were now coming in sharp ragged motions, her sweet yet coffee-laced scent whispering over his mouth and seeping into his pores, but still she made no effort to kiss him back.

And nor did she push him away or tell him to stop.

And nor did she push him away or tell him to stop when he found the hem of her top and slipped his hand under it.

The texture of her skin was silkier and softer than he remembered, as if some benevolent creator had wrapped her in satin.

Needing to kiss more than just her mouth, he dragged his lips over her cheeks and jaw then made a trail down her neck, the scent of her flesh firing into senses already fit to burst.

He was fit to burst. Never—*never*—had he

felt sensation and heat like this and it was everywhere in him, from his heart that battered against his ribs to his loins that weren't aching, they were burning.

And never had he felt he would give all his worldly goods to receive just one kiss.

Carrie was letting him kiss her. She was letting him touch her. But she was giving nothing back. She was clinging onto that last ounce of stubborn denial for dear life.

But still she didn't push him away or tell him to stop.

He brushed his lips over her mouth again and nuzzled his nose against hers. His hands swept over her back then moved to her belly, which quivered under his touch as it had when she had kissed him on his veranda. She jolted again when his fingers brushed the underside of her breast, her own fingers tightening reflexively on his arm, but this time she made no attempt to escape.

For a moment he thought fevered wishful thinking had imagined her rubbing her pelvis tighter to his until he heard her swallow between the shallow breaths and her fingers tighten on him again.

Cradling her head in his hand, he tilted her back a little to stare deep into her eyes.

She stared back mutely, everything those

stubborn, beautiful lips wanted to say, everything she was feeling reflecting back at him.

Wordlessly he brought his other hand up to her throat then slowly dragged it down, over the breasts he longed to touch without a barrier, feeling the heavy beats of her heart through it, skipping over her quivering belly, down her thighs until he could reach no further and he gathered the material of her skirt into his fist. Then, working slowly, he brought it up to her knee before letting the skirt go so it covered his hand, which now rested on her bare thigh.

Her left hand still gripped his biceps, her right hand…

Her right hand was now splayed on his abdomen, the heat from her touch penetrating through his shirt.

Andreas gritted his teeth. He wanted nothing more than to escape the straightjacket his clothes had become but instinct told him to wait just a little longer…and Carrie pressed her pelvis into his again, her body making spasmodic movements, her lips parting as if readying herself for his kiss again…

He obliged, covering her mouth with his. He felt the lightest of movement beneath it before she clamped her lips back together and turned her head to rub her soft cheek against his. Her fingers on his abdomen had slipped around to splay across his back in short grabbing motions.

He traced his fingers further up her thigh until he found the heat he was seeking and brushed his thumb against the damp, burning cotton.

She jerked against him, the hand holding his lapel moving up and gripping his neck. When he slid his hand under the cotton and found the damp, downy hair that covered her most intimate secret, she jerked again and pressed her cheek even tighter against his.

He slid his fingers lower and discovered her in full bloom, the feminine complement to the painful constriction in his underwear.

Closing his eyes to everything but this moment, he breathed her in as he continued to touch her, finding a rhythm with his fingers that had her grinding against him, her breaths so shallow and rapid he couldn't distinguish where one breath started and another began until she flung herself tightly against him and buried her face in his neck, crying out. Shudders rocked through her frame as she clung to him, her breaths rapid and hot in his neck.

Andreas, his cheek pressed into her hair, now had both arms wrapped around her, stroking her back.

And she held him tightly too.

'Don't say it.' Her words were spoken into his neck but then she shifted and loosened her hold on him, disentangling herself to cup *his* face with *her* hands. Dark, ringing hazel eyes beseeched him. 'Please, don't say it.'

He gave a short, sharp shake of his head. Blood roared in his ears, his chest the tightest he had ever known it.

Even if she hadn't asked, he couldn't look at her and smugly say, *See, I knew you wanted me.*

That had been the most erotic, mind-blowing and…*touching* moment of his life, and he would never diminish it.

Her eyes still gazing into his, she swallowed then slowly brought her face closer and covered his lips with her own.

It was the sweetest, most tender kiss of his life.

And then her lips parted, her tongue danced into his mouth, her arms locked around his neck and he was kissing her back with all the passion his soul possessed.

Carrie shut off the part of her brain shouting at her in increasingly terrified shrill tones to stop this madness *now*.

She shut it down completely.

She had never felt so alive, had never known her body capable of such intense, concentrated pleasure.

He had done this to her. Andreas. His touch, his scent…him. It was as if every part of her body had been tuned to a frequency only he had the dial to.

She had fought her desire with everything she had and it hadn't been enough. He'd broken through her resistance completely. And now she wanted the rest of it and she wanted him to have the pleasure he had just bestowed on her too.

He tasted so darkly masculine, she thought headily, as she drank in his kisses and razed her fingers up and down the nape of his neck. Why fight something that felt so right? Just what was she scared *of*?

But she had to shut her mind off again when the shrill voice tried to break back through to tell her exactly what she was scared of.

She was giving her body to Andreas, nothing more. Nothing more…

For the first time in her life she was going to let her body guide her. Consequences only happened when people allowed foolish dreams to overtake their reality.

Dimly she was aware of him gathering her tightly to him and lifting her off the worktop.

Later, she would have no concrete memory of them getting to a bedroom, just floating images of being carried in his arms and them falling onto the nearest bed in a tangle of limbs.

Their eyes locked.

Carrie lifted her top up and over her head, discarding it without thought.

His throat moved before he held out a hand.

With fingers that fumbled with inexperience, she undid his shirt buttons. As soon as she had the first three opened she put her lips to his chest and breathed in his clean musky scent, a pulse rippling through to her core when he groaned. His skin felt so smooth yet so different from her own, hard where she was soft and so very warm. Brushing her lips all over his chest, rubbing her cheek against the fine hair covering much of it, feeling his raging heartbeat thrum through his skin, she worked the rest of the buttons until the shirt was undone and Andreas shrugged it off, then his arms wrapped around her waist to undo her bra. He flung it away and sat back to stare at her naked breasts for the first time.

His eyes dilated, a moan dragged from his throat. He raised a hand that belied the faintest tremor and cupped her.

A bolt of need pulsed through her, so pure and so shockingly strong that she snapped her eyes shut and struggled for air.

Breasts that had always just…been there, a part of her like her arms and legs, suddenly felt heavy and swollen and needy. He massaged them gently then replaced his hand with his mouth.

She gasped and clenched her hands into fists.

All those wonderful feelings he had brought about in her such a short time ago were building up again but this time they felt so much more, the need being evoked no longer concentrated but *everywhere*, every part of her aching for his touch and yearning for his kiss.

As if he could sense her need, Andreas stripped off the rest of her clothes, trailing hot moist kisses all over her flesh, increasing her hunger.

Her skirt was unbuttoned and pulled off, thrown to the floor, the plain cotton knickers quickly following and then she was naked, lying fully exposed to a man's gaze for the first time in her life.

Andreas stared down at her, his eyes a colour she had never seen before, dark and molten. He'd removed his trousers—how, *when*?—and now all that was left to remove was his underwear.

Not taking her eyes from his, Carrie sat up to kneel before him and placed her hands on his heavily breathing chest. She dragged her fingers slowly down, over the hard muscles of his abdomen, to the band of his snug-fitting grey boxers.

Swallowing the moisture that had filled her mouth, she gripped the band between her fingers and tugged them down over his hips.

Released from its tight confines, his erection sprang free.

She swallowed again, unable to hide her shock.

The glimpse she had seen when he'd been in the bath...that had been nothing to seeing it loud and proud in the flesh. She'd already gauged that he was well endowed but had been unprepared, not only for his size but also the unexpected beauty of it.

She looked back into his eyes and drank him in, a languid, floaty feeling seeping through her. *How could it have been anything but beautiful when it belonged to the most beautiful man in the world?*

The molten eyes seemed to drink her right in too. He took her hand and brought it to his lips, then gently lowered it down to his erection, holding her loosely enough that she could snatch her hand away if she wanted.

She did not want to snatch it away, she thought dreamily. She *wanted* to touch it. Tonight, she wanted everything.

Letting him guide her, she took it into her hand and felt it throb beneath her fingers.

He moaned, his throat moving.

With his hand covering hers, showing her without words how he liked to be touched, she followed his lead. Thrills raced through her to hear his tortured groans and see the ragged movements of his chest. She could feel the heat bubbling inside her, every bit as turned on with what she was doing and the effect it was having on him as she had been when he'd been touching her.

She didn't hide her disappointment when he suddenly pulled her hand away.

He speared her hair and brought his face to hers to growl, 'I want to come inside *you*.' And then he kissed her, a kiss so deep and passionate she felt her bones turn to heated liquid.

The kiss was over all too soon as he pulled away from her and climbed off the bed. Stepping out of his boxers, he grabbed his trousers and pulled out his wallet. From it, he removed a small box of condoms.

He flashed her a tortured grin. 'I have been living in hope, *matia mou*.'

He was back by her side on the bed before she could blink.

He dropped the box on the pillow and pinned her down beneath him, kissing her again, her mouth, her cheeks, her neck, his hands roaming her body, muttering words she didn't understand into her ear but which added to the sensations already consuming her. The weight of his erection lay heavy on her thigh and she made to touch it again but he grabbed her wrist to stop her.

'Later,' he whispered hoarsely. 'You can do whatever you want to me later but right now I need to be inside you.'

She kissed him, sweeping her tongue into his mouth, letting him know with her body how badly she needed him inside her too.

It didn't matter that this was something she had never done before. She hadn't done *any* of this before, had spent her adult life denying herself something so beautiful and…*necessary*. Not any more.

Keeping his body so deliciously flush on hers, he groped for the packet and quickly extracted a square foil from it, which he ripped open with his teeth. Then he shifted slightly onto his side and deftly sheathed himself.

His mouth found hers again as he twisted back to lie on top of her, using his thighs to nudge her legs a little further apart so his erection was right there…

He entered her with one driving thrust, plunging her straight into a world where heaven and hell collided.

Hell; the sharp pain she hadn't expected and that made her suck in a shocked breath…and which Andreas either felt or sensed because he stilled.

'Carrie?' He lifted his head a little to look at her, confusion appearing in the molten depths of his eyes.

But already her body was adjusting to the feel of him inside her, the pain already diminished.

She smiled and tilted her chin to press her mouth to his. For long moments they simply touched lips together and breathed each other in. Then she closed her eyes as he began to move, and then...

Then she found herself in heaven.

He made love to her slowly, his thrusts tempered. His hands held hers tightly as he ground his groin against hers, stimulating her as he filled her.

Yes, she had found heaven.

Then he raised himself onto his elbows to lock eyes with her, causing the stimulation to deepen in rhythm with his deepening thrusts. Sensation pulsed like bolts of lightning in her core, a burning need growing and intensifying.

Wrapping her arms tightly around him, she ran her hands down his back exulting in the feel of his muscles and sweat-slicked skin beneath her fingers, then closed her eyes to everything but the sensations taking control, submitting to them, submitting to the pleasure and magic of everything they were creating together until the lightning exploded.

Pleasure shattered through her like a tsunami, bolts tearing down her spine and into her every crevice with an intensity that sent white light flickering behind her eyes and a cry from her mouth that sounded distant with the drumming in her ears.

Electricity danced on her and through her, almost stunning her. She held onto Andreas as if he were an anchor in this world, a dim acceptance that this was all because of him and only him, that there could never be another...

His lips crashed onto hers as he gave a roar that seemed to have been dredged from his very soul and drove into her for one last powerful thrust that made him shudder with the force of his own release.

Shocked eyes fell on hers before he gave one last groan and lowered himself onto her with his full weight, and buried his face in her hair.

Carrie tightened her hold on him, sighing to feel his breath tickling her scalp.

The sensation that had erupted through her with such violence was now a gentle ripple and she closed her eyes, wishing with all her heart that she could bottle this moment for eternity.

CHAPTER TEN

ANDREAS AWOKE ON his side to find Carrie's face pressed against his chest, an arm and thigh slung around him.

He also awoke to find himself fully aroused.

He took a deep breath and rolled onto his back, careful not to disturb her sleep. She rolled with him, her face now buried in his side, her hand drifting to rest on his abdomen.

The room was shrouded in such darkness he knew without having to look that he'd slept for many hours. He smiled ruefully to know he'd done that most male of male things and fallen asleep almost immediately after sex.

Yes, a most male of male things but not something he had ever done before. But then, he had never known sex to be like that before, an experience so intense that climaxing had felt as if his brains might explode from his head. He'd made it to the bathroom to dispose of the condom then fallen back into bed, scooped Carrie into his arms to cuddle against her, and fallen straight into blissful sleep. The evening had still been light outside.

He'd never done that before either: fallen asleep with his arms wrapped so tightly around someone.

He had good reason to believe Carrie had never done any of this before.

The little spot of blood he'd seen on the sheets when he'd climbed back into bed had only consolidated what his body had told him when he'd first entered her.

Carrie had been a virgin.

He hadn't bedded a virgin since he'd lost his own virginity. Then, they had both been seventeen and full of raging hormones. He'd promised faithfully to marry her if she slept with him, a blatant lie told by horny teenage boys the world over. They'd given each other their virginity and afterwards he'd ridden off on his scooter, cigarette dangling from his mouth, feeling like a king.

He smiled at the memory. He hadn't thought of Athena for years. She'd dumped him for one of his friends a few weeks later, which he was sure had broken his heart for at least five minutes. As far as he knew, Athena and Stavros were still married with an army of children running them ragged.

He was quite sure she was the last virgin he'd been with. The irony of him actually marrying the second virgin he slept with after promising to do that faithfully with the first did not escape him.

He ran a hand gently over Carrie's hair, smoothing it, enjoying the silky feel of it on his skin.

What had made her wait so long?

To have missed out on those heady teenage years where hormones dictated every part of your life? No office romances either? He kept a strict hands-off rule with his staff but he didn't expect them to keep their hands off each other. So long as it didn't interfere with their work he couldn't care less what the consenting adults he employed got up to.

Had Carrie been waiting for someone special?

He brushed his finger along her cheek, his chest tightening to imagine the myriad reasons why she had chosen to remain a virgin and what the implications for them were.

She stirred against him and nuzzled into his chest. Her movements were enough to tighten the other, much baser part of him that had already been wide awake and aroused and when her fingers began to drift lightly down his abdomen…

Minutes later and he was inside her again.

* * *

Carrie was awake for a long time before she dared move. She was pretty sure she had the huge bed to herself. The heat that had enveloped her throughout the night had gone.

Eventually she plucked up the courage to slowly roll over and confirm what her instincts were telling her.

Andreas had left the room.

She stared at the indentation on his pillow and was horrified to find tears filling her eyes.

Quickly she averted her gaze to the ceiling and breathed raggedly through her mouth, a hand on her chest, blinking frantically as she fought the tears back.

What had she done?

Oh, dear God, what had she *done*?

She had slept with him. Not once, but three times.

She had become someone new in his arms. She'd felt like a beautiful butterfly that had emerged from its cocoon for the very first time and found its wings.

Andreas had taken her to paradise but now, with the early morning light streaming through the shutters, paradise seemed as distant as the moon. Now she wanted to find her old cocoon and crawl back inside it.

What was the protocol for dealing with this?

Was there a protocol lovers kept to when seeing each other for the first time after making love?

Lovers?

Heat suffused her everywhere and she covered her face with both hands, fighting back the sobs desperate to break out.

She didn't want to be Andreas's lover. She didn't want to be anything to him, not his fake fiancée, not his fake wife, not anything...

The door opened.

As quick as lightning, she turned back onto her side and squeezed her eyes shut.

If she pretended to be asleep maybe he would leave her alone.

Footsteps padded over the floor tiles. New scents filled the room. Coffee. Fresh bread.

She heard another door slide open and cool air filled the room.

A minute later the bed dipped. A hand brushed against her hair.

She couldn't stop her shoulders moving in reflex at his touch.

Holding her breath as tightly as she held the sheets around her, she rolled onto her back.

Andreas was sitting on the edge of the bed wearing nothing but a pair of jeans.

His eyes were on her, a wariness underlying the intensity of his stare. 'Good morning,' he said quietly.

She managed the semblance of a smile but couldn't get her throat, echoing with the vibrations of her hammering heart, to move enough to speak.

'I've got breakfast for us,' he said after an impossibly long period of silence between them during which they did nothing but stare at each other. 'It's on the balcony.'

She hadn't known this room had a balcony.

She didn't even know what room they were in. It certainly wasn't the one she'd been given.

'Give me a minute to get changed and I'll join you out there,' she whispered.

His eyes narrowed slightly before he nodded and got to his feet.

She watched him step out onto the balcony, sliding the glass door shut behind him. Only when he was out of her eyeline did she slide out of the bed and snatch her discarded clothes from the floor. She found the en-suite and locked the door behind her.

Barely twelve hours ago she had felt not a modicum of shyness in showing her naked body to him. He had kissed and touched every single part of her and she had thrilled at the sensual pleasure of it, a pleasure she had never imagined; seductive and addictive.

She had been drunk with it all. Drunk on Andreas.

Now she wished for nothing but to hide back in her protective cocoon and forget it had happened.

Throwing her clothes on, she splashed her face with water and smoothed her hair as best she could with her fingers, trying not to look too hard at her reflection in the mirror so she couldn't see the bruised look of her lips or the glow on her skin that had never been there before.

Andreas was eating a Greek breakfast pastry when she joined him on the balcony.

'Coffee?' he asked amiably.

'Yes please.' She sat opposite him and looked at the huge spread laid out between them. 'Did you do all this?'

'Of course not. I called the chefs in and got them to make it.' The mockingly outraged face he pulled as he said this, that *How dare you even suggest I soil my hands by preparing my own food?* expression, tickled her and she found herself fighting back a grin.

But then she met his eye and the smile formed of its own accord. Not a full grin, but her lips loosened enough to curve a touch.

His features relaxed to see it. He pushed her cup of coffee to her then leaned back. 'Eat something. You must be starving.'

That reminded her of their missed dinner. And his roses...

'What's wrong?' Andreas asked, seeing her brow suddenly furrow.

'Those poor roses. I never...' She dropped her gaze from his and snatched a bread roll, opening it with her fingers.

He knew exactly what had caused her face to look as if she'd been dipped in tomato juice and his loins twitched to remember lifting her onto the worktop, the roses abandoned, and all that had followed.

And what had followed had been one of the best nights of his life. Maybe the best. He couldn't think of a better one.

'The housekeeper has revived them,' he assured her, remembering the way Carrie had rubbed her nose against the petals when she'd taken them from him.

She'd rubbed her nose over his stomach in the exact same way...

The twitch in his loins turned into a throb, the memory of her nails digging into his back as she'd orgasmed strong enough that he could feel the indentations on his skin as fresh as if she were making them still.

'That's good,' she said, nodding a little too vigorously. She stretched for the jar of honey with a hand that trembled and said in a voice so low he had to strain to hear her, fresh colour smothering her entire face, 'Does she know I, err, we, slept in the wrong room?'

'It doesn't matter, *matia mou*.'

'She needs to know.' She struggled to remove the lid. 'When we're gone someone else will stay here. The sheets...'

'Carrie.'

She stopped talking and reluctantly met his gaze, eyes shining with what looked suspiciously like unshed tears, her chin wobbling.

She'd been a virgin.

Until twelve hours ago she had reached the age of twenty-six untouched.

He could not shake that thought from his mind.

'Let me open that for you,' he said gently, nodding at the honey jar clasped so tightly in her hand.

She pushed it across the table to him, her shoulders slumping.

He twisted the lid off and pushed it back to her, resisting the urge to force her to take it from his hand.

She had been a virgin.

She had never made love before.

She had never faced a man the morning after before.

The vulnerability he had seen in her when he'd given her the flowers was even more starkly apparent now and it tugged at his heart to see it and with it came a compression in his chest, an overwhelming punch of emotion he couldn't begin to comprehend but which set alarm bells ringing inside him, a warning that he was steering into dangerous territory and it was time to back away.

'There is no wrong or right room here because the villa is mine,' he said in as even a tone as he could manage.

She darted a little glance of gratitude at him before dipping a teaspoon into the honey jar. 'What do you mean?'

'I signed the paperwork for it yesterday. That's where I went after I dropped you here, to meet with the previous owner.'

'You bought it? But why?'

He shrugged. 'I was looking for a villa to rent for the week. I didn't see anything I liked so I looked at villas for sale and this was available.'

'You bought a villa on a whim? Without even looking at it?' She spread the honey on her roll.

'I saw the pictures. I know the island pretty well—I've had an eye on buying something here for a while. I knew it was in a good location with plenty of privacy. Why not?'

'You already have a holiday home.'

'This will not be a holiday home for me, not like my property in the Seychelles. I can work from here. Agon is a prosperous, independent country with a growing economy. It has many residents looking to invest their cash. It is close enough to fly or speedboat to Athens. It has staff familiar with the house and I get to speak my native tongue for a change. It ticks all the boxes and best of all it has year-round sunshine.'

'Why do you run your business from London?' she asked. 'You clearly hate the city.'

'I don't hate it. In the summertime it is beautiful but the rest of the year it is so grey and dreary. I grew up with the sun on my back. But to answer your question, London was never my first choice to run my business from. When I was younger I wanted to live in America. That's why I went to university there. I had many ideas in my head about what America was like and assumed it had year-round sunshine like my home in Gaios.' He grinned, remembering his youthful naivety and lack of geography skills.

Her lips twitched with humour as she took a bite of her honey-slathered roll.

The tension in her frame was loosening.

'The winters in Massachusetts came as quite a shock, I can tell you,' he continued. 'When I graduated from MIT I was offered a job with an investment firm in Manhattan who were offering an obscene amount of money for a graduate. As you know, that's when my parents were on their knees, financially speaking, so I took the job, worked hard and built many contacts so I could strike out on my own, and tried not to freeze to death in the dire winters. When I started Samaras Fund Management, my intention had been to build the American side up then set up European headquarters in Athens. London and the other European capitals would have been subsidiaries. I'd reached the point where I was earning serious money, my parents were in reasonable health and settled in their new home...'

'Did you buy it for them?' she interrupted, eyes alive with curiosity.

'As soon as I could afford it. They didn't want to stay in Gaios any more, which I could not blame them for after the way they had been treated by the people there, so I brought them a house on Paros. We all thought the worst of what life could throw at us was over and then my sister and brother-in-law died.'

Carrie sucked a breath in.

Andreas said it so matter-of-factly that if she hadn't seen the flash of pain in his eyes she could believe his sister's death had meant nothing to him.

'It was carbon monoxide poisoning, wasn't it?' she asked softly.

He nodded, his jaw clenching. 'They were

on holiday celebrating their wedding anniversary. The apartment they were staying in had a faulty boiler.'

She remembered reading the inquest report and wanting to cry for Natalia, their orphaned daughter, a girl Carrie had welcomed into her home and loved fiercely. Violet hadn't been the only one hurt when Natalia stopped staying at their home. Carrie had missed her too, missed the sunshine the girl had brought to their home.

In the year before the expulsion it had been rare for Violet to be at home without Natalia. Had that been why Carrie had failed to see how badly off the rails Violet was falling, because Natalia's cheerfulness and sweet nature had masked it?

But hadn't Carrie herself noticed the sunniness in her demeanour wilting those last few months before Violet's expulsion? A strain in both girls' eyes she had put down to teenage hormones.

Natalia had been so comfortable in their home. She would make herself drinks if she was thirsty, help herself to cereal if hungry…

Natalia would never have dropped Violet like a stone if something major hadn't occurred. If she'd wanted to keep seeing Violet she would have done; not even a strict uncle could have kept her from making contact if that had been what she wanted.

But she hadn't wanted to contact Violet because Andreas had been speaking the truth.

Violet had tried to seduce him, had punched Natalia in the face and blamed Andreas for her expulsion in revenge and, Carrie deduced, her mind ticking frantically, ice plunging into her veins, because she hadn't wanted to admit to the one person in the world who loved her that she had bought the drugs herself, and admit what she was becoming. An addict.

Violet had lied to save face and for misplaced revenge against the man who'd rejected her advances. Her vengeance was misplaced because the man she'd truly wanted to get back at, namely the vile specimen who had taken her virginity on her sixteenth birthday, had become unreachable. In Violet's mind at that moment, Andreas had been interchangeable with James; two rich, handsome men of a similar age. The expulsion, her desperate, wanton behaviour in the months leading to her expulsion...

Caught in her reckless heartache, Violet had managed to discredit herself without even trying. No one in their right mind would believe her story about the fabulously rich, media-friendly James Thomas grooming and seducing her. No one other than her big sister.

The ice in her veins had moved like freezing sludge to her brain.

Carrie had never followed a story without some initial proof. Violet had produced plenty of proof against James; blurry photos on her phone taken slyly when he hadn't been looking and screenshot messages—he'd been clever enough to insist on using apps where messages deleted themselves after being read but not clever enough to guess a lovestruck teenager would still find a way to save them.

There had been no proof against Andreas. Not a shred.

Carrie had gone after him on nothing but her damaged sister's word and that word had been a lie.

'Carrie?'

She blinked and looked into the eyes of the man she had tried to ruin.

'Are you okay? You are very pale.'

How could he even bear to *look* at her, never mind with concern?

She could still feel his touch on her skin, his kisses on her lips. He had made love to her as if she were the only woman in the world.

He should hate her.

He probably *did* hate her.

She hated herself.

What she had done…

Her chest had tightened so much it hurt to draw breath.

She needed to speak to Violet, she thought, as fresh panic clawed at her chest. There was still the chance Carrie might be wrong. She couldn't condemn her sister without giving her the chance to defend herself.

'I'm fine,' she managed to say. 'I was just thinking of Natalia.'

And I was thinking that you are not the monster I've been telling myself you are for the past three years.

This conversation they were having…

Andreas had started it to calm her down.

He knew she'd been a virgin. He'd known it the moment he entered her. He could have chosen to embarrass her about it and demand to know why she, a seemingly confident twenty-six-year-old woman, had spent her adult life as a singleton.

Instead he had given her a way to face being with him without making her burn with humiliation.

'Did you move to London for her?' she added.

He gave her another narrow-eyed unconvinced look before nodding. 'My sister used to read all those wizarding books to her. Natalia thought all boarding schools were like that and asked if she could go.' He smiled though his eyes saddened at the memory. 'I could afford it so I offered to pay the fees for any school my sister thought suitable. They chose London. I bought Tanya and Georgios a house close to the school so Natalia could spend weekends with them. When they died I moved to London and kept Natalia at her school. I couldn't put her through any more disruption.'

So he had uprooted his own life instead and moved to a city he didn't particularly like with a climate he hated.

'Is that what you meant when you said you'd spent fifteen years waiting for your freedom and that another six months wouldn't make any difference? Because you'd had to make your parents your priority and then your niece?'

'Natalia is at university, my parents are happy and settled and have all the home help they need... Now I want to spend as many of my days as I can where the sun shines and live my life as I please.' The wolfish grin she'd once so hated but now tugged at her heart curved on his lips, the gleam returning to his eyes. 'And if delaying my freedom for another six months means I get to see your beautiful face every day then it will make the delay a little sweeter.'

She swallowed. 'How can it be sweet when I tried to destroy you?'

'Because living with me is the price you have

to pay to put it right. When it is over we will be even.'

'And last night?' The question was out before she could take it back.

He gazed into her eyes a long time before answering. 'Last night was nothing to do with you putting things right. I make no apologies for desiring you and you should make no apologies for desiring me. Attraction is bound by no rational thought. I have wanted you from the minute you stepped into my office and my bedroom door will always be open to you. If you enter is up to you.'

The meaning in his eyes was clear.

Andreas would make no further move on her.

If their marriage was to be more than a piece of paper she would have to be the one to instigate it.

It was a thought that should make her feel safe but didn't. Not in the least.

One thing Carrie did know for certain, required no proof or corroborating evidence for, was that with Andreas her feelings were like kindling.

One touch and she turned into fire.

CHAPTER ELEVEN

ANDREAS'S NEWEST STAFF were true professionals. He'd taken Carrie out shopping in an exclusive enclave in Agon's capital, where an arcade of designer boutiques and chic cafés resided, tiny compared to London and Paris's exclusive areas but with staff who could smile without looking as if their bottoms were being sucked out of their cheeks and who treated their clientele as if it were a pleasure to serve rather than a chore.

When they'd returned to his newest acquisition late afternoon he'd found the garden transformed exactly as he'd asked before they'd left and the scent of charcoal filling the air.

'I thought you said you couldn't cook,' Carrie said accusingly when he'd added the two juicy steaks onto the newly built brick barbecue.

She was sitting at the garden table, lithe legs stretched out, wearing a strapless mint-green summer dress and a cream wrap around her shoulders to stave off the evening chill.

His senses told him she wore no bra under that dress.

'I can burn meat as well as any caveman,' he replied with a grin. 'Why don't you make yourself useful and get a bottle of wine from the fridge?'

'Because I'm not your skivvy any more?' she suggested.

'Do you not feel guilty that I'm doing all the work while you are sitting there doing nothing?'

'Nope.' She looked pointedly at the bowls of salads and rice that had been prepared for them by his new chefs and laid on the beautifully presented table.

The staff had all gone now.

'Please?' he asked pointedly.

She pretended to consider then got to her feet. 'Okay, then. Which wine do you want?'

'There's only one variety in the fridge.'

She bounded off into the villa, a spring in her step he'd never seen before.

It occurred to him that her jest about not being his skivvy any more had been the first time she'd alluded to those few days when he'd had her at his beck and call.

They had been on Agon for only three days and the change in her had been incredible. Yesterday they had explored Agon together, admiring the island's rich heritage and what Andreas considered to be the most beautiful palace in the world. They'd eaten out, their conversation light and non-confrontational but the wariness he'd been greeted with at breakfast had still vibrated from her rigid frame. She avoided his gaze. The few times their eyes had met colour had suffused her face and her top lip would pull in. When they'd returned to the villa she had mumbled a goodnight before disappearing— fleeing—to her bedroom.

He hadn't touched her once and he hadn't flirted with her either.

He wanted to make love to her again. He hadn't thought it would be possible to want it more than he had before but that was how it was, a constant ache, a constant fizz in his blood, a constant awareness of her every movement but her virginity had changed everything.

If they were to make love again Carrie had to make the first move. He needed to know that what they were sharing came from her head as well as her body.

Today, she had greeted him at breakfast with a smile that had been undoubtedly genuine.

That smile had pierced into his chest.

When he had taken her shopping for a dress to wear for his cousin's wedding, he'd prepared himself for a fight. When he'd explained, keeping his tone even, that she was only attending the wedding because of him and therefore it was only right he pay for her dress she had taken him by surprise by actually agreeing.

She hadn't let him buy her anything else though, and he hadn't argued the point. Carrie had a fierce independent streak he admired even if he did find it infuriating. He no longer found it insulting. There was a reason for it and sooner or later he would discover what that was.

She reappeared with the wine at the exact moment he judged the steaks to be cooked.

At the table he put the steaks on their respective plates and sat down, reaching for the wine.

She surprised him again by allowing him to pour her a glass. The only alcohol she had shared with him had been his Scotch the night the truth had come out.

He held his glass out. *'Yamas.'* At her blank expression, he said, 'It means good health.'

She chinked her glass to his and took a sip of her wine. Her eyes widened a touch. 'I'm not a big fan of white wine but this is nice.'

'I should hope so for the price I paid for it,' he said drily. 'I have it imported directly to all my homes. This crate arrived while we were shopping.'

She had another sip. 'This really is lovely. And you have it imported to *all* your homes?'

He shook his head self-mockingly. 'I don't

take drugs, I no longer smoke…good quality wine and Scotch are my only vices.'

'You used to smoke?'

'Something else your investigations into me didn't reveal?'

As he finished the question with a wink, Carrie couldn't help but smile.

She could hardly believe they'd reached a place where they could *joke* about her attempts to investigate him. Both of them.

It was all down to Andreas. He'd rumbled her, had his fun while he punished her, then insisted she marry him to put things right but he wasn't holding a grudge. He wasn't one to hold a grudge but that, she suspected, was because he didn't need to. If a problem arose he fixed it straight away with whatever means he thought necessary.

He was no angel but by no means was he a monster like most of the rich men she'd dealt with through the years. When he wanted something done he expected it to be done immediately, patience was not his strong point, but he wasn't spoilt. Considering the wealth he'd accrued he was surprisingly grounded.

'I smoked when I was a teenager. I was obsessed with everything American and old seventies movies where the cool heroes always smoked and rode motorcycles. I wanted to be

Steve McQueen.' He burst into laughter. 'The closest I could afford to a motorcycle was a beaten-up old scooter but cigarettes were easy to come by. I thought I was the coolest kid in Gaios, driving around on that pile of junk without a helmet and a cigarette hanging from my mouth. I turned my poor mother's hair white.'

His self-mockery and evident amusement were infectious and Carrie found herself laughing at the image he'd painted.

When she had set out on this endeavour she hadn't suspected for a minute that Andreas could be such good company. Their one conversation on the phone all those years ago had been short and to the point, his tone what you would expect if speaking to a bank manager. That one time she had seen him outside the headmistress's office he'd oozed menacing power. He'd frightened her.

Yes, Andreas had a dark side but she had come to realise that it only came out when people he loved were threatened.

What would it be like to be loved by this man…?

She would not allow her thoughts to go down that road.

Andreas was rich and powerful. He had charm and looks. He was everything she hated, everything she feared.

But he'd been honest about everything. He wanted his freedom. What they were sharing here, now, was pure circumstance. What she felt for him was a result of the forced proximity she'd been thrown into. When this was all over she would walk away. She wouldn't give this strange chemistry another thought. He would be out of sight and out of mind.

But right here and now he was in her sight and completely filling her mind.

Putting her knife and fork together, she pushed her plate away, put her elbow on the table and rested her chin on her hand. She'd eaten half of the steak he'd cremated for her but had no recollection of it, too caught up in listening to Andreas's staccato voice. 'You sound like you were a right tearaway as a child.'

'I was the bane of my parents' life,' he admitted unrepentantly, 'but also the apple of their eye so I got away with murder.'

'I was a good girl.'

'Really?' He topped their glasses up with more wine.

'Do you have to sound so surprised?'

He studied her as he sipped his wine, his own plate pushed aside too. 'No. I am not surprised.'

'Because I was a virgin?'

There. It had been said. The elephant that had parked itself between them had been acknowledged and the knot in her stomach loosened because of it.

The knot had become like a noose.

'It doesn't suggest a wild past,' he said slowly, his gaze on hers as he put his glass to his lips.

'I never had the chance to be wild,' she admitted. 'My mum was diagnosed with cancer when I was thirteen. I had Violet to look after—she's seven years younger than me—so I guess I supressed any teenage hormones that might have been primed to unleash. I comfort ate a lot. I never felt comfortable in my skin. It's funny because my mum was *beautiful*. Honestly, she was stunning. She'd be hooked up with drips and machines all around her and the doctors would flirt with her. Mind you, she flirted with them too. Men loved her.'

'Were you jealous of her?'

'No.' She shook her head as she thought about it. 'No, I felt sorry for her. She was married twice and had a string of boyfriends. None of them treated her well.'

'And you thought all men were like that?'

'No. I just thought she had terrible taste in men.'

Andreas laughed into his wine but his eyes read something other than amusement. There was compassion there, and something baser, the same something that had been there from the very start.

Carrie hadn't spoken about her mother for a long time and it felt good to do so now, brought her memory alive. Her darling mother had been a princess in Carrie's eyes, a woman who adored her two daughters and never shied from showing her love for them.

'There are some good men out there,' she said softly, staring into the hypnotic gaze that no longer frightened her. The meaning she read in it...it was nothing that she too didn't feel. She wanted Andreas, with a burning yen that had seeped into her soul. 'My grandfather was a good man. He was poor. Humble. Not flashy like the men my mother went for. She was like a magpie, always wanting the shiny pretty things. She could pick a rich man at ten paces and have him eating out of her hand with the flutter of her eyelashes.'

'So your father is a rich man?'

'Actually, he was the only poor one. He didn't even have a job—they were at school when they got together. Mum gave birth to me when she was seventeen.'

'You were an accident?'

'My mum always said I was the best accident in the world.' She would say it while planting kisses all over Carrie's face and tickling her ribs until they were both crying with laughter.

Andreas listened to Carrie open up about her life, watched those plump lips talking, feeling as if he had a fist pushed against his chest, pressing against his heart. Her hazel eyes shone in a way he had never seen before, her love for her mother shining through, dazzling him.

What would it be like to have those eyes shining with love for you…?

'They married when they discovered she was pregnant but split up not long after I was born,' she continued in that same, slow cadence, those shining eyes fixed on him, an openness in them he had never seen before. 'My dad moved away after they split up so I've never seen much of him but he's always remembered my birthday and makes a point of visiting a few times a year. I've always known he loves me.' A look of mischief flittered over her face. 'He's head gardener at the real Hargate Manor.'

He burst into great rumbles of laughter at this unexpected twist. 'It is a real place?'

Her lips puckered with sheepish amusement. 'I've been there a couple of times. It's a beautiful estate.'

Andreas drank some more wine and continued to stare at her. She mesmerised him. She'd mesmerised him from the moment she'd stepped into his office.

'*You're* beautiful,' he said throatily.

She tilted her head and smiled, a smile that stole his breath and made a man feel he could fly to the moon. 'You make me feel beautiful.'

A long, breathless moment passed between them as he gazed into eyes that shone with a hundred emotions.

Then she straightened, put her hands on the table and pushed her chair back.

She stood up, the wrap that had covered her shoulders sliding off and falling into a puddle at her feet. She didn't notice, a whole range of emotions flittering in hazel eyes that burned into him.

Slowly she trod towards him.

The air between them thickened in those few small movements and by the time she stood before him it crackled.

Andreas could no longer breathe.

Two elegant hands cradled his cheeks, delicate fingers rubbing against his skin. She leaned forward and pressed the tip of her nose to his.

Her eyelids closed and she breathed him in then her lips brushed his.

'You make me feel beautiful,' she repeated in a murmur into his mouth. The sweetness of the wine mingled with the sweetness of her breath and seeped right into his airways and through his veins.

Carrie had a taste that had been designed for him.

And it was *all* for him, he thought, the thickening in his loins a weighty ache. No other man had tasted her sweetness. And no other man would…

'You make me feel like a woman,' she whispered before her lips closed around his and she was kissing him, deep scorching kisses, her fingers sliding to cradle his head, everything a mimic of the night she had kissed him in the Seychelles but everything new.

This time there was no restraint. No pretence, no holding back, no hate, no anger.

Just two people with an unquenchable thirst for each other.

In one motion, he gathered her to him, pulling her onto his lap just as he had what seemed a lifetime ago and as he felt her bottom press into his lap, raw hunger slammed into him.

In a flurry of ravenous kisses her soft, pillowy breasts crushed against his chest, Carrie's fingers raked over his neck, over his shoulders, her nails scraping over his shirt, her hot tongue trailing over his cheeks and jaw, tasting him, her teeth biting into his skin, delicious jets of pleasure igniting everywhere.

And he touched her back with equal fervour, roaming his hands over the hot flesh that quivered and burrowed closer into him at his every touch, as if she were trying to burn their clothing off through willpower alone.

Somehow, with her chest crushed so tightly to his, she found the buttons on his shirt and opened them enough to burrow beneath the material to find his bare skin. Her fingers splayed all over his chest, nails raking his skin, scorching a trail of burning heat over him with her touch alone, her mouth devouring his again, her breaths shortening.

His mouth found her neck and he inhaled her earthy yet delicate scent, that erotic, womanly smell that was Carrie's alone.

When she found the waistband of his trousers, she didn't hesitate to tug at the button but when she couldn't undo it, cupped her hand over the tightly compressed erection and squeezed over the material.

He groaned into her neck at the constrained pleasure her touch there unleashed, then licked all the way up to her chin and her mouth.

Her eyes were open yet hooded. If a look ever had the power to make him come without a touch, the look ringing from her eyes would be it.

Holding her tightly, he lifted her in one motion and sat her on the table so he was standing between her parted thighs.

She stared at him, desire vibrating from her, then tugged the top of her dress down to her waist.

She wore no bra.

Her plump golden breasts shone under the rising moon. Spearing her hair as he cradled her head to support her, he lowered her back then dipped his head to take one of the pebbled nipples into his mouth.

The gasp that flew from her mouth turned into a moan as he slavered her with his attention, kissing, nipping, licking.

Her legs hooked around his waist, gyrating herself closer to him, her ankles digging into his buttocks as her back arched, her need for him as beautifully obvious as the emerging stars above them.

When he ran a hand over one of her clinging thighs and slid higher to her buttocks, he was the one to moan when he found her hot and damp. She jerked against him, trying to find whatever relief she could get.

Abandoning her breasts, he kissed her hard on her mouth and she matched it, a violent fever spreading between them as he pinched the sides of her knickers with his fingers and she raised her bottom to allow him to pull them down to her hips.

With one final clash of mouth and tongue, he then tugged her knickers down her legs and past her pretty feet, threw them onto the floor and removed his wallet from his back pocket. As he took the square foil out, Carrie returned to undoing his trousers, this time unbuttoning it with one flick of her fingers and tugging the zip down.

As he took the condom out of its wrapping she tugged his trousers down his hips, freeing his erection.

There was not a moment of hesitation.

Andreas slipped the condom on in one deft movement, hooked an arm around her waist to pull her to him, and thrust himself inside her.

Tight and hot, she welcomed him, pulling him deeper inside her, the look in her eyes as he stared into them sinking him deeper into her spell.

She slipped a hand around his waist and up his shirt, her nails biting into his skin, urging him on, their lovemaking hot and frenzied, tender and hard all at the same time, and then she was grabbing his buttocks to drive him even harder into her, mumbled, sensual words flying incoherently from her lips until her head tilted back. A ragged cry escaped her mouth and then she was thickening around him, clinging to him and Andreas found himself slamming headlong into the ecstasy of his own release, brighter, sharper and more intense than anything he had ever known before.

As he held her protectively, waiting for the shudders vibrating through both their bodies to lessen and the heavy beats of their echoing hearts to subside, a fierce possessiveness grabbed at his chest, words floating in his head he couldn't shake.

Carrie was his.

CHAPTER TWELVE

CARRIE APPLIED HER mascara for the third time and willed her hand to stop shaking and poking the wand in her eye.

The nerves she was feeling were almost as bad as when she'd waited in the reception room to be taken in to Andreas for the first time.

His cousin was getting married in three hours. Andreas had gone to collect his parents and niece from the airport and drop them at the hotel where the evening reception would be held. The whole family was staying at the hotel, Carrie and Andreas included. Apparently it was a Samaras tradition for the bride and groom to have their first breakfast as a married couple with their family all looking at them and knowing exactly what they'd been getting up to in the marital bed.

Thank goodness she and Andreas were marrying in a Chelsea registry office. It would be just them and a couple of witnesses.

She was terrified of meeting his parents but even more scared of seeing Natalia again. It scared her even more than having to pretend to everyone that she and Andreas were in the throes of a whirlwind love affair.

A whirlwind lust affair she could easily fake, mainly because that wouldn't involve any fakery.

She could hardly keep her hands off him.

She didn't know exactly when the shift in her thinking had occurred, just knew that as she'd changed for dinner after their shopping trip, she'd looked in her mirror and asked herself what she was so afraid of. Why fight something so pleasurable? Why deny them both? She'd slipped her dress on and closed her eyes, remembering his touch on her skin.

Carrie had discovered the joys of sex. Twenty-six years of a dormant libido had been unleashed and now her body was making up for lost time on all it had missed out on.

She told herself that on an hourly basis.

The good news was that she had a full six months to get all this making up out of her system because she couldn't quite quell the fear that her body only reacted this way because of Andreas. *For* Andreas.

But as she also continually told herself, if it was only him she reacted this way to, then so what? It was still only sex, glorious, blissful sex.

Ta da. Her make-up was done. Third time lucky.

Her phone rang.

She grinned to remember how Andreas had deliberately kept her incommunicado when she had first infiltrated his life. It was one of the reasons he'd chosen to take her to the Seychelles, because the signal on his peninsular was so dire.

Her grin dropped when she saw her sister's name flash up.

Carrie had left three messages for her in the past week. She'd bitten back the hurt to find herself being ignored again. Violet had always been good at ignoring her if she didn't want to speak.

Taking a deep breath, she answered it. 'Hi, Vee. How are you?'

Silence.

'Are you there?'

'Is it true?'

Carrie's heart sank. 'Is what true?'

'That you're seeing Andreas Samaras.'

She took another deep breath. 'Yes. It's true.'

And it's all because of you and the lies you told.

'You know what he did to me, right?' After only three months in California her sister had picked up an American twang.

'Violet... Are you still seeing the counsellor?'

'Answer my question.'

'I will when you answer mine. Please, tell me you're still seeing him.'

'Her. My counsellor's a her.'

'I'm sorry. I thought you were seeing a man.'

'I was.' The stiff angry tone suddenly changed. Became softer. 'We decided I would find it easier to talk to a woman.'

'And are you finding it easier?'

'Yes.' She sounded surprised. 'I am. She's really nice and non-judgemental.'

Carrie tried not to take that as a dig against herself. 'I'm glad.'

'Now you answer my question. You know what that man did to me?'

'He didn't do anything to you, did he, Vee?' she said gently, her heart thumping, mouth dry. 'He didn't do what you accused him of. He didn't set you up. The drugs were yours. Vee, it doesn't change how I feel about you. I still love you.'

All that played in her ear was silence but she knew her sister was still there.

'I'm sorry you felt you couldn't trust me enough to tell me the truth but please, I beg you, admit the truth to yourself. Talk it through with your counsellor. You were treated terribly by James but Andreas isn't James. He is nothing like him.

'Violet… I love you. I forgive you. Now, please, find a way to forgive yourself.'

This time the silence on the other end was the silence of a disconnected line.

Violet had hung up on her.

'Was that your sister?'

Carrie jumped and spun around.

She hadn't heard Andreas come in. Normally she was very attuned to his movements around the villa but she had been so engrossed with her one-sided conversation with Violet that she hadn't heard him return.

He was standing in the doorway, his black tuxedo on minus the jacket, a sombre expression on his handsome face.

She nodded.

'What you said…you believe me.'

She nodded again.

'Since when?'

'Since you told me,' she whispered before hanging her head in shame. 'I just couldn't admit it. Violet is my Achilles heel. She always has been.'

He paused before asking, 'Why is she seeing a counsellor?'

'Because she's a drug addict.'

Suddenly she could hold it in no longer. She slumped onto her dressing room chair and burst into tears.

The tightness Andreas had experienced when he'd listened to Carrie say she believed him, to hear her defending him, became a tight ball to see her dissolve before his eyes.

These weren't tears, these were racking sobs, each one tearing his soul.

In three strides he was before her, crouching on his haunches to cradle her head on his shoulder, stroking her back, her tears soaking through his shirt.

It was a long time before the sobs lessened and she removed her face from his shoulder and wiped it with her hands.

Red-rimmed hazel eyes fixed on him and she inhaled deeply. 'My sister is a drug addict. She is in recovery in America, living with her father because one of her drug dealers beat her into a coma when she couldn't pay her tab.' The tears filled her eyes again, spilling over to race down her cheeks, shoulders shaking. 'She nearly died. My baby sister nearly died.'

Stunned at this revelation, Andreas took a moment to process it.

'That bastard didn't just seduce her. He fed her drugs. He gave an innocent girl a drug addiction.' She covered her mouth then dropped her hand as she gave a long, ragged exhalation. 'I must have been blind. I had no idea how bad her addiction was until a few months after her expulsion.' Her lips made a little grimace of distaste. 'I found her in bed with a much older man. There were drugs on the floor…she denied it but I knew she'd had sex with him in exchange for the drugs. She had no other money. Her father had cut her allowance off when she got expelled; she'd been able to afford her own until then. I was only a recent graduate and not earning very much. She had no money and absolutely refused to get a job.'

He got to his feet and ran a hand through his hair, kneading his scalp. 'Why wasn't she at school?'

'Because she'd been expelled,' she reminded him.

'I know but she could have gone to another school after she'd taken her exams.'

'She wasn't allowed to take them.'

Anger coiled in his gut. 'The headmistress promised me Violet could sit them.' He had insisted on it.

'Then she lied to you. Violet wasn't allowed to set foot in that school again. I tried to arrange for her to sit the exams somewhere else but she refused. She gave up on life. She'd stay out all hours and never let me know where she was, then turn up steaming drunk and high as a kite, often cut or bruised from fights she'd got into and I'd patch her up and pray it was the last time I had to put ice on her face or sleep on her floor because I was terrified she'd choke on her own vomit, but it never was. She was arrested God knows how many times, hospitalised, had her stomach pumped… I honestly thought she was going to kill herself.'

Andreas sat heavily on the bed facing her, his heart pounding.

Carrie's beautiful golden skin had paled as she'd relayed this tale of horror that no one should ever have to live through, and to think his beautiful Carrie had been the one to live it made his guts coil again in fresh anger and self-loathing at the part he had unwittingly played in it.

After a few moments of silence, her eyes found his and she continued in a voice so low he strained to hear.

'I watched her try and kill herself for three years and there was nothing I could do to save her, and I tried *everything*. I locked her in her room; she smashed the window and jumped out. I staged numerous interventions with professionals; she just laughed in our faces. I even flushed a bagful of her cocaine down the toilet and got a punch in the face for it.' She gave a shaky laugh. 'Natalia has my sympathy. I know what a mean right hook Violet has.'

'Carrie…'

'No, please, whatever you want to say, just let me say this first. I believed Violet's lies that you set her up and I listened to her drunken ranting about you in the same way she would drunkenly rage about James and not once did I question them. As a journalist, you would think I would have had the sense to verify it all first, and I want you to know I am sorry for believing that about you and for all the lies I told in some stupid, futile, *dangerous* attempt at revenge. I could have caused your business and reputation untold damage and I am truly ashamed of myself. I think… I think I lost my mind.'

It was all true, Carrie realised bleakly as she spoke her confession.

She didn't need to verify Andreas's version of events. She knew the truth in her heart.

'What you have had to deal with these last three years would cause anyone to lose their mind,' he said quietly.

'It wouldn't cause you to lose yours,' she said with certainty. 'I don't think anything would ever cause you to lose your mind.'

'I came close when my sister and brother-in-law died,' he admitted. 'I couldn't fix that. All the other stuff my family and I had had to deal with before then, it was all fixable, even my parents' health issues. However bad things got, there was always hope. Tanya and Georgios's death…what hope was to be found there? But then you know all about that with your own mother.'

She nodded. 'Death is the one thing that can't be fixed, isn't it?'

'It's the finality,' he agreed. 'One minute they are there the next they are gone and all that's left are the memories. But I had Natalia to care for just as you had Violet after your mother died and...

'Why is Violet living with her father now?' he interrupted himself. 'Why wasn't she living with him before? I always assumed she was an orphan.'

'She might as well have been an orphan for the time he gave her. Raymond, Violet's father, divorced our mum and moved to America years before Mum died. When she did die he didn't want Violet—he had a nice new nubile wife and was living the childless dream. We agreed that he would continue paying for Violet's education—did I tell you he was also rich?—and that she would become a weekly boarder so I could concentrate on my studies, but that she would live with me at weekends and holidays. He gave us both an allowance for it to work.' Her smile was bitter. 'When it came to money, his generosity was limitless.'

'And that's when you became Violet's guardian?'

'Yes. He handed his twelve-year-old daughter's welfare into my nineteen-year-old hands and washed his own hands of the pair of us.'

'*Theos.*' He gave a low whistle. That was the same age Natalia was now. He'd been a grown man of thirty-one when he'd become Natalia's guardian. 'I didn't realise you were so young when you became her guardian. And her father didn't want her? No wonder she went off the rails.' He shook his head, unable to comprehend how a man could turn his back on his own child. Natalia wasn't even his and he knew he would lay down his life to protect her. 'Why is she with him now when he didn't want her before?'

'I blackmailed him.'

He found himself smiling. 'Really?'

She met his eye and matched the smile. There was no joy in either of their curved mouths. 'I'd been begging him for years for help and he kept fobbing me off and fobbing me off. She almost died from that beating, Andreas. She was in a coma for three days. Something in me went ping. I didn't even think about what I was going to say, I just phoned him and said if he didn't fly over and see his daughter and finally take responsibility for her then I would publish a photo of Violet's battered body on the Internet and tell the world he'd refused to help her.'

'And that worked?'

'He arrived the next day. A week later he flew

her back to America with him. I don't know why I hadn't threatened it before but I'd spent so long just getting through each day, caring for Violet, plotting my revenge on you and James…' She winced. 'Sorry.'

'It is okay.' He slid off the bed and knelt before her. Taking her hand in his, he kissed the palm. 'No more apologies. I'm the one who is sorry. I should have told you, not the school…'

'You did the right thing.' Carrie squeezed the hand holding hers so tenderly. 'You were protecting Natalia. Violet would have been expelled sooner or later. She was using drugs on school property. They would have noticed eventually.' She shrugged then took a deep breath. '*I* should have noticed. I should have seen what was happening to her—I *did* see—but I didn't know what I was seeing. Does that make sense?'

'Carrie…' He raised himself up and put a hand to her neck and pressed his forehead to hers. 'You must not blame yourself. None of what happened to her is your fault. You have put your life on hold to raise her and to save her. She is nineteen now, yes? The same age you were when you became her guardian. You have given her all the support and help you can, you have avenged her against the monster who first steered her on this awful path. You can do no more. I heard you say to Violet that she has to forgive herself. You must do the same and forgive yourself too.' Kissing her forehead, he moved back and rubbed his thumbs under her eyes.

The motion made her remember the make-up she must have ruined with all her tears and she let out a cry. 'Your cousin's wedding!'

'It doesn't matter.'

'It does. We need to go.'

His brow furrowed and he stared intently into her eyes. 'Do you feel able to? I can make an excuse if you would rather stay.'

'No. They are expecting us.' She blew a long breath out and gave a wobbly smile. 'We have a wedding announcement of our own to make. You would look very strange doing it without your fiancée by your side.'

'Are you sure?'

How could she be anything but sure? She would do whatever was needed to kill the whispers against Andreas's business and his reputation. That was a mess of *her* making, no one else's.

Andreas was a good man who had put his life on hold for his family, just as she had for her family. A good, generous man who didn't deserve to have his reputation smeared by rumours and innuendoes. He deserved to spend the rest of his life living it with the freedom he'd had denied him for so long, and in six months he would be able to do just that. He could hop from country to country as he pleased, for work and pleasure, however he saw fit. He could drink Scotch in a palm-lined bar until the sun came up, he could bed all the women he wanted without worrying about being a bad influence on an impressionable teenager…

A hot red pain pulsed in the centre of her brain at this thought and she slammed her palm to her forehead.

'Are you okay?'

She heard the concern in his voice and quickly forced a smile.

Where had that pain come from?

'Yes, I'm fine. Just imagining how badly my face needs repairing from all those ugly tears.'

He stroked her cheek. 'Your tears are not ugly and your face just needs a clean.'

'Give me five minutes.'

He nodded and got to his feet before helping her to her own. Then he took her head in his hands and kissed her. It was gentle and fleeting but with so much tenderness in it that for one awful moment she thought she might cry again.

CHAPTER THIRTEEN

Andreas's driver joined the procession of cars lining up to enter the church's car park. There seemed to be some issue with one of the cars—an engine failure if Andreas was to guess correctly—and nothing was moving.

He could see his parents and niece standing at the front, chatting happily with the dozens of other guests. Both his parents had many siblings so family weddings were always large, noisy affairs.

Carrie was looking out of the window at the exuberant greetings taking place too. 'Why did you buy a holiday home in the Seychelles rather than closer to your family?' she asked, turning to face him with a wrinkle in her forehead. 'The way you speak of them—you clearly adore them.'

He looked down at their entwined fingers then back to her face. She'd cleaned herself up and put on only a little make-up. Her eyes were still a little red but he doubted anyone else would notice. She still looked ravishing in her long, off-the-shoulder cream silk dress with subtle blue leaf prints.

'I wanted a bolt-hole away from them all,' he admitted. 'My parents only like to travel short distances. The Seychelles is too far for them.'

And he'd thought he was done with family.

Not *done* done, just his time for some distance whenever he wanted to escape but…

'I was preparing myself for my freedom. I have been planning it for two years now, since Natalia told me she was going to medical school and I could see my freedom from responsibility waving a flag at me.'

His heart-rate began to accelerate, blood racing to his head, staring from Carrie to his family, his family to Carrie, Carrie to his family.

His father had just whispered something in his mother's ear, lovingly squeezing her seventy-four-year-old waist.

Andreas thought of the longevity of their marriage, and all they had been through, all the ups and downs, all the highs and lows.

Why had he thought having the freedom to see and do whatever he liked was better than having someone he loved to share all the experiences with?

He had a sudden vision of him and Carrie, forty years from now, surrounded by their own grown-up children...

Children?

He had long stopped wanting children. He'd raised a teenager he loved as if she were his own and had been so certain, so damned *adamant* he didn't want to go through it again...

'I can't do it,' he said suddenly.

'Do what?'

'Introduce you to my family as my fiancée when we don't mean it. I cannot marry you knowing it isn't true. I cannot make false vows.' And as he said the words aloud, he knew them to be true, and a weight he hadn't felt on his shoulders lifted.

Somewhere, somehow, he had fallen for his poisonous viper of a journalist.

He could laugh at his old notions about her.

There was nothing poisonous about Carrie. Prise off the shell she carried herself in and there was a kind, loving, independent, fiercely protective woman. When Carrie loved someone, it was with everything she had. She loved with her whole heart.

And he loved her with the whole of his.

'Oh.' She had gone very still beside him.

He tugged the hand he was holding to his

mouth and pressed his lips to the knuckles. 'Marry me for real.'

'*What?*'

'I am serious. Marry me. For real. Not for six months.'

'No.'

'Carrie…'

'The answer is no.' She pulled her hand from his and shifted away so her back was to the door, staring at him warily as if he were a dangerous dog that could bite. 'I agreed to six months. You can't change the terms now.'

'I am not changing the terms. I am telling you I cannot go through with the terms we agreed on. It would not feel right.'

'Why not? Is it because I was a virgin so you feel honour-bound to keep me for ever?' She spoke slowly, not taking her eyes from his face.

'It has nothing to do with you being a virgin. I admit, I like knowing I'm the only man you have been with…'

She gave the briefest of smiles, one that did not reach her wary, watchful eyes. 'Your sexist undertones are coming out.'

'I am being honest with you and I say *this* with all honesty too—you could have slept with a hundred men and I would still be asking you to marry me for real.'

In the few, intense weeks they had been together they had seen the worst in each other and the best. She had slipped so effortlessly into his life it was as if she had always been there.

'Okay.' She dragged the last syllable out then nodded her head. 'Well, I am telling *you*, with all honesty, that I will not commit to anything longer than six months.'

'Why not?' he challenged.

'You have to ask? The whole reason I am here is to put right the awful wrong I did to you but that shouldn't mean I have to give up my whole life...'

'Do you not feel anything for me other than a debt you need to pay?' he asked, forcing his voice to stay even, not wanting to jump to conclusions. They had done that enough already...

But if they hadn't jumped to their prior conclusions about each other they wouldn't be sitting there now...

And he wouldn't be feeling as if he'd started swimming only to find the water had turned into treacle. The shell he had so carefully prised open was reforming around her. He could virtually see the seams knitting themselves together.

'Are you telling me I have imagined everything that has happened between us?'

'No, I'm not saying any of those things.' There was an air of desperation in her voice.

'You can't just throw something like this at me and expect me to fall in line with it.'

'I don't want you to fall in line.' He took a deep breath and pinched the bridge of his nose. 'How long do you want to have?'

'Six months.'

'I mean how long do you want to think about it?' he asked through gritted teeth.

'I don't need to think about it.' She pulled her knees up to her chest and hugged them tightly. 'We marry for six months and then we divorce and I move back into my London house and you live the life you've been dreaming of.'

'I don't want that life any more. Being with you…it has…not changed me but made me see I want someone to share it all with.'

'Oh, so you want a constant companion while you live the high life and I'm here and available and you've got to marry me anyway so I'll do? How am I supposed to do that around work? Or am I expected to give up my job?'

'Did I say *any* of that?' he demanded, the anger clawing in his guts finally finding a vent.

He wouldn't say he'd expected her to agree to his proposal on a whim but he'd thought—in as much as he'd thought about it, which he hadn't really considering he'd only just accepted his own feelings for her—she would at least be receptive to the idea.

He acknowledged his own lie to himself.

His feelings for Carrie had been like a runaway train from the minute she'd stepped into his office. He'd thought it had been the same for her.

Had he *really* got it so wrong?

Had the closeness they'd developed really just been a figment of his imagination?

'Six months of marriage where we live in London then you can relocate your headquarters to Athens and I stay put. That's what we agreed,' she said obstinately.

'What if I were to offer to live permanently in London with you? For ever.' He laid his challenge down.

'The answer is still no. I do not want to marry you. Don't you get that? I will pay my debt. I will do six months. And then I will leave.'

'How can you be so cold?' he asked in disbelief. 'I am offering to give everything up for you and you…'

'Cold?' she interrupted. Suddenly she leapt from her perch on the seat and pushed him back so she was on top of him, pinning him down, her little hands holding his wrists above his head, her snarling face above his.

She'd moved so quickly he'd had no time for defence. If the situation were more humorous and less of a feeling that everything was fraying at the seams, he would have admired her ninja skills.

'Don't you call me cold!' she shouted. 'Don't you dare! I have spent my life caring for the people that I love and losing them. I nursed my mother for six years and then she was gone. I have loved and cared for Violet her entire life and what good did that do? She's gone too! She is lost to me. I would give my entire life to have them back so don't you dare call me cold and don't you dare ask me to commit the rest of my life to a man who's been yearning for his freedom and would only break my heart. Yes, Andreas, *you*,' she spat. 'If our marriage was for real you would bore of me in months; that yearning for freedom would still be in you getting stronger and stronger and then what would happen? You'd get your chequebook out and pay me off like all rich men do when something nicer and newer grabs their attention.'

Andreas stared into her spitting eyes and felt the very coldness he'd accused her of creep into his veins.

Everything made sudden gut-aching sense.

He twisted his wrists easily from her hold and snatched her hands, pulling them together to hold her wrists in one hand while he levered himself up with his free hand.

Then they were staring at each other, enough hate and poison swirling between them to choke on.

He had been wrong about her. Prise her shell off and she was still just a poisonous viper of a journalist.

'Oh. I get it,' he said slowly. 'You still think I'm just a rich bastard who is pre-programmed to cheat and treat women like dirt.'

Her eyes widened. Suddenly the fury went from them and she blinked rapidly, shaking her head. 'No. No, sorry, I didn't mean it like that. I know you're not like other...'

'You have said enough,' he cut in icily, then he dropped her wrists and banged on the dividing window. 'I'll get out here. Take Miss Rivers back to the villa to collect her belongings and then take her to the airport.'

He turned back to stare at her now pale face for the last time. 'I will arrange for my jet to take you back to London. Your debt to me is over.'

Then, without a word of goodbye, he got out of the car and strode through the other idle cars to his family.

Carrie watched him walk away, her heart in her mouth, loud drumbeats banging in her head. The scratchy panic that had torn her insides into pieces as Andreas had spoken of marriage had gone and all that was left was a numbness, as if she had been anaesthetised.

She rubbed her wrists, the look in his eyes as he'd let go of them, discarding them as if they were trash, right there in her mind.

Andreas had looked at her as if she were a toxin.

He merged into the merry crowd outside the pretty white church without once looking back.

A separate merry crowd had gathered together to push the broken-down car away. She watched them as if through a filter, seeing but not seeing, Andreas's hateful look the only thing she could picture with clarity, as she sat there too numb to take anything else in.

He had never looked at her like that before. Not even when the truth had first unravelled itself.

She was barely aware of her own car moving until the driver made a slow U-turn in the space that had opened up before them and crunched away from the happy wedding party, just as Andreas had made a U-turn on their plans…

Their plans?

There were no plans now, she realised, her heart hammering more painfully than it had ever done.

Their relationship, such as it was, was over. *They* were over.

She was still too numb to do more than swallow back a huge lump that had formed in her throat.

Andreas sipped at his single malt as he read through the emails Debbie had decided were worthy of his attention, keeping one eye on the time. An old friend from his Manhattan days, when he'd been a mere employee, was due any minute. As was their tradition, they'd agreed to meet in their old 'watering hole', as Frank still liked to call it.

'Can I get you another drink, sir?'

He looked up from the screen at the young, pretty waitress who had been paying him extra attention since he'd arrived at the bar and settled himself in an empty corner booth. It was still early but tonight was the opening game of the baseball season and this bar was a firm favourite for Yankee fans. He estimated that he and Frank would have an hour of catching up before the place filled up.

'I'm good for the moment, thank you,' he answered with a quick grin. 'I'll let you know if I need anything else.'

She winked before sashaying away. 'Be sure that you do.'

Focussing his attention back on his smartphone, he rubbed the back of his neck and chided himself for wasting an opportunity for a little flirtation.

This pretty waitress was a perfect example of what he'd been looking forward to all these years: grabbing opportunities for fun when they came along. Andreas was now free to do what he liked with whom he liked when he liked. Natalia had announced at his cousin's wedding that she was moving in with her boyfriend. A boyfriend she had conveniently forgotten to mention to her protective uncle until she was certain things would work out between them.

He'd wished her luck and even managed to inject sincerity in his voice.

Who knew, he thought cynically, taking another sip of his Scotch, maybe it would work for them? And if it didn't he would be there to pick up the pieces. He'd come to accept that when it came to Natalia, he would always be there.

The main thing, he had told himself numerous times, was that his freedom had officially arrived. He didn't even have a fake fiancée to worry about.

Lord knew what he would do if the rumours about him gained traction. It had been six days since he'd shut the door on the viper and their relationship. He'd ordered Debbie to check in frequently with their media contacts and inform him immediately if the rumours started up again. So far, all was quiet.

Maybe their brief relationship had been enough on its own to quell the rumours.

The waitress caught his eye again. She really was incredibly pretty, a true all-American girl with a toothy smile and perfectly blonde hair.

Carrie's hair had been blonde the first time he'd met her, their first oh-so-fleeting glance…

He took a deep breath and downed his Scotch. *Do not think of her. Not by name.*

It was easier to depersonalise her. Depersonalise her and forget about her.

Less than a minute after he'd slammed his empty glass on the table, the waitress brought him another over.

'Where are you from?' she asked, lingering at the table.

'Greece.' He returned the smile and willed himself to feel something.

Anything.

'Greece, huh? I've always wanted to go there.'

She'd moved close enough for him to smell her perfume. It was nice. Floral.

It did nothing for him.

Carrie's scent had been evocative. It had hit him in the loins.

His mind suddenly loosened, memories he'd shut tightly away springing free. The heat of her kisses, the movement of her lips when she spoke, the way she smiled sleepily when she looked at him after waking…

The way she had cried on his shoulder, her desolation over her sister, the way she had clung to him, as if he were the lifeline she'd needed when her emotions had thrown her out to sea…

Carrie…

Carrie…

Carrie!

Her name rang loudly in his ears.

'What's your name?'

'Carrie.'

'Sorry?'

He blinked and saw the waitress looking at him with puzzlement.

He'd said her name aloud.

Carrie.

Scared, terrified Carrie who'd spent her life watching her mother and sister being used and sometimes abused by rich men.

Her kisses didn't lie. Her lovemaking didn't lie.

Her scared brain did.

'Her name is Carrie,' he said more clearly. 'The woman I love. She's called Carrie.'

He hadn't told her he loved her. He'd held that back as the strength and vehemence of her rejection had accelerated, protecting his ego.

Why had he not recognised the fear in her eyes for what it was rather than just listened to what she'd said? Why had he not laid his heart truly on the line for her?

The reason for that was simple. As this pretty waitress would no doubt say, the reason was because he was a shmuck.

He got to his feet, pulling a couple of twenty-dollar bills from his wallet, and thrust them into the waitress's hand. 'If a tall bald man called Frank asks for Andreas, tell him I remembered I had to be somewhere else.'

Hurrying out of the bar, he hailed the first cab that came his way and instructed the driver to take him to the airport.

CHAPTER FOURTEEN

CARRIE CLOSED HER laptop after her video chat with her sister feeling slightly lighter.

They had just shared their first real, meaningful conversation since Violet had confessed to her affair with James.

Violet had done as Carrie had beseeched and confessed her lies about Andreas to her counsellor. It had been at the counsellor's behest that Violet had arranged the video chat.

Seeing her sister's face on the screen, in real time, had been almost as good as the conversation itself. She'd put on weight, no longer the gaunt stick-thin figure who could still fit in children's clothes. Her complexion was clearer too, although the effect of that was to highlight the scars that had accumulated on her face over the years. Raymond had promised that he would pay for treatment for the scars once she had been clean for a year.

The man who'd been such a scummy, negligent father had finally come into his own and was doing the right thing by his daughter. He'd even come to the computer and waved at Carrie, which she'd conceded was a big deal for him considering the last time they'd spoken she'd been blackmailing him.

In all, things were looking good. Much more positive.

The only dark cloud had come when Violet had asked how things were going for Carrie with Andreas. When Carrie had responded with a prepared airy, 'It fizzled out,' Violet had been crestfallen.

'I thought you'd be pleased,' Carrie had said, trying her hardest to keep things light.

Violet had bitten her lips in the exact same way their mother had done. 'I just want you to be happy,' she'd blurted out.

'I *am* happy,' Carrie had promised, her stomach wrenching.

Violet had not looked convinced.

All week Carrie had kept her airy face on, telling curious colleagues that yes, she and Andreas had had a brief romance but that they had decided it wouldn't work between them long term.

Her only real gulp-inducing moment had been when the features editor had asked when she would have the exclusive interview written up. She'd forgotten all about that.

She opened her laptop back up and decided to write the feature now. She had no transcripts of any of their conversations but she knew if she started, they would come back to her.

She would write it, email it to Andreas for his approval—after all, everything they had discussed had been between the two of them and not for public consumption—and if he agreed, she would send it to the features editor. If he refused she would say he'd pulled out. She would take the blame for it. Happily. She would not have his name tarnished.

Even if he did hate her.

She caught sight of the time and saw it was almost one in the morning.

It was Saturday.

This was supposed to be their wedding day.

She took a long breath and opened a new document to write on.

The time didn't matter. She'd hardly slept more than a couple of hours a night since her return to London.

The nights had become her enemy, a time when her brain did nothing but try to think of Andreas.

And now it was time to slay his ghost. Finally allow herself to think about him properly, write the feature and then spend the rest of her life forgetting about him.

Oh, but the pain in her chest. It *hurt*. Really hurt. It was as if someone had punched her right in her heart.

So she started writing.

She soon discovered she didn't need transcripts.

Every minute of their time together had lodged in her brain.

Every shared conversation had committed to memory.

Andreas Samaras's fortune came about almost by accident, she wrote, her fingers almost flying off the keys as she wrote about the terrible time when his parents' business had gone under and how it had been the spur he'd needed to work as hard as he could to save them from financial ruin.

The more she wrote, the clearer it became, the clearer he became, emerging from a picture in her mind so he might as well be standing right there, in front of her. If she stretched out a hand she'd be able to touch him.

His life. His selflessness.

Everything he'd done had been for his family. His great wealth couldn't insulate them from tragedy but it ensured his parents never had to worry and his niece could train as a doctor without the usual student encumbrances. His extended family had benefitted too, aunts, uncles, cousins, all either having their mortgages paid off or new homes bought for them.

No member of the Samaras family would ever struggle financially while Andreas was alive.

Five hours later, her hands cramped, hot pains shooting up her arms, she stopped, exhausted, and burst into tears.

For the first time she admitted to herself what she had thrown away.

She hadn't meant to cast him in the same torrid light as those other rich men who had abused their power. She had been long past that, had long accepted Andreas was nothing like those men.

His proposal, his idea they should marry for keeps, hadn't just taken her by surprise but terrified her. She'd already been feeling raw after spilling her soul to him and had panicked.

He'd never said that one word she'd longed to hear from his lips, the same word that also would probably have made her dive out of the window.

At no point had he mentioned love.

But she had never given him the chance. She had said no without even having to think.

No, I will not marry you properly. No, I will not take the chance of us finding happiness together because I'm a big scared, distrustful baby who requires proof.

What proof could he give her that their marriage would last and that he would never cheat or break her heart? None, because that proof didn't exist! He had no crystal ball or time portal.

And neither did she.

All she could do was trust her instincts and her heart, and both were telling her—*screaming* at her—that she had made the biggest mistake of her life.

Andreas had offered her his world but she'd been too scared to take it from him.

And now it was too late.

Shoving her laptop so hard it fell off her desk, Carrie buried her face in her hands and wept.

It was too late.

Too, too late.

Andreas banged hard on the blue front door for the third time.

Still no response.

Pushing the letterbox open, he crouched down. 'Carrie? Please. Open the door. Please.'

'She's gone out.'

He spun round to find an elderly woman walking a small dog up the neighbouring front path.

'Did she say where she was going?'

The woman shook her head as she rummaged in her pocket for her keys. 'She went out when

Trixie and I went for our walk. Half an hour ago or so.'

'Did she say when she was coming back?'

'No. She was all dressed up so I wouldn't think she'll be back soon.' The woman opened her door then looked at him one last time. 'If you're thinking of robbing her place, I'd be very careful. She has a very noisy burglar alarm.'

Despite the situation, he couldn't help but grin. 'Noted.'

The door slammed shut.

With a heavy, defeated sigh, he slumped down onto Carrie's front door step and cradled his head in his hands.

He would just have to wait until she came back from wherever she'd gone *all dressed up*.

Carrie rarely dressed up. She was always, always elegant, but never noticeably dressed up. The only occasion she had properly dressed up for had been his cousin's wedding, the day everything had imploded between them.

That had been a week ago.

He looked at his watch. Half past one. Their wedding was supposed to take place in half an hour…

His brain began to tick.

Had Carrie cancelled the registry office? Because he hadn't…

And just like that, he was on his feet, racing

past his idling driver, pounding the ground to the nearest Tube station, racing down the stairs, yanking his bank card out and waving it at the turnstile, pausing only to check which line he needed to take before racing to the platform.

People of all shapes and sizes were clambering onto a train and he joined the throng.

He hadn't used the Tube in years but this was one occasion where speed trumped luxury. He hardly noticed the people jostling into him. He certainly didn't care.

Four minutes later and he was in Chelsea, following his nose to the registry office, checking his watch constantly until, with five minutes to spare, he was there and racing up the stairs to the waiting room outside the room he'd booked for their service.

The waiting room was empty.

He doubled over, partly from exertion but mostly from grief.

The cramp in his stomach spread to his chest and clenched around his heart.

The pain was indescribable.

What a fool he was.

He'd allowed hope to override common sense. What on earth had he been thinking?

Why would Carrie have come here? She'd made her feelings perfectly clear but he, egotistical fool that he was, had been unable to accept the truth and had....

'Andreas?'

He froze.

Slowly he straightened before turning around.

The door to the officiating room had opened. Standing at the threshold, clearly on her way out, stood Carrie, the registrar hovering behind her.

She stared at him as if she'd seen a ghost.

The neighbour had been right that she'd been dressed up. She wore a knee-length summery cream dress and a soft cream leather jacket. On her feet were cream heels.

The only colour on her were her eyes. They were red raw.

'What are you doing here?' she whispered.

'What are you doing here?' he countered, not trusting what his eyes were telling him.

Silence hung over them as they gazed at each other, Carrie drinking in the tall figure she had resigned herself to never seeing again.

She'd told herself she was running a fool's errand but that hadn't stopped her rifling through her wardrobe for the most bridal-type clothing she could find.

She'd fallen into bed, utterly exhausted, at six in the morning and after three hours' fitful sleep had woken with a cast-iron certainty that she had to get herself to the registry office.

Even now, with what looked and sounded like Andreas standing in front of her, she couldn't say where this certainty had come from. It had been a compulsion that had taken over her.

She'd made it to the registry office well before the appointed time and had watched one happy couple and two dozen happy guests pile into the room, then pile out twenty minutes later.

During those twenty minutes she had waited on her own.

When the last guest had gone and her reality had come crashing back down on her, she had burst into fresh tears. The registrar had been sympathy itself, taking her into the room and making her a cup of tea, giving her the time she needed to gather herself together in privacy rather than have her humiliated should anyone come into the waiting room while she was wailing.

And now, as she looked at the ghost before her, a scent played under her nose, a fresh, tangy cologne that had her bruised heart battering against her ribs.

She gazed into the light brown eyes she loved so much, saw them narrow with the same disbelief that must have been ringing in hers then saw the truth hit him at the exact same moment it hit her.

In seconds, he'd hauled her into his arms and was kissing her fiercely as she clung to him, inhaling his scent, more tears spilling from her eyes and splashing onto his face.

It was *him*! Andreas was there! He had come.

'I'm sorry, I'm sorry, I'm sorry,' she cried, raining kisses all over his face, hungrily inhaling more of his scent, tasting his skin…

It really was *him*.

Eventually he disentangled their clinging bodies to take her face in his hands and stare at her.

There was a wonder in his face. 'You are here. Oh, *matia mou*, you are *here*. I didn't dare believe…'

'I'm so sorry,' she said, tears falling over the fingers cradling her face with such tenderness.

'No, my love, it is I who is sorry. My pride—my ego—never let me say what was in my heart.' His words came in a rush. 'I want to marry you for ever because my heart will not accept anything less. I love you. You are the bravest, most loyal and loving woman I have ever met. You are stubborn and sexy and I love everything about you. The only freedom I want is the freedom to wake next to your face every day for the rest of my life, so please, I beg you, marry me. I love you. I can't be without you.'

Carrie covered his hands with her own feeling as if her heart could burst. If it did, glitter and starlight would explode over them.

'I love *you*, Andreas, and I'm so sorry for...' she raised her shoulders helplessly '...*everything*. You are the best person I know. You're sexy and funny...the way you have taken care of your family... I should never have... I was scared.'

'I know.' He covered her mouth with his. 'I need to learn patience. You know what I'm like. I want something and I want it *now*. You need to think things through. I have to accept our brains work differently.'

She laughed softly into his lips. 'I'll teach you patience if you'll teach me spontaneity.'

'It's a deal.'

Their kiss to seal their deal was broken by a loud cough.

They broke apart to find the registrar looking at his watch, a faint smile on his lips. 'If we're going to marry you we will have to do it now, I'm afraid. We have another wedding party due any minute and my colleagues who are supposed to be acting as your witnesses have other duties to attend to.'

Andreas looked at Carrie. 'Well? Do you want to do it?'

She kissed him. 'I'm here, aren't I?'

The brightest, most dazzling grin she had ever seen broke out on his handsome face. 'Then let's do it.'

So they did.

And neither of them ever regretted it.

EPILOGUE

'YOUR VEIL IS falling off!' Natalia screeched as Carrie attempted to get out of the limousine.

'I don't know why I agreed to wear the stupid thing,' she said in a mock grumble.

'Because you want to make an old woman happy… Violet, can you hold your side still for me?'

Between them, Carrie's two bridesmaids fixed her veil then both inspected her face one last time before the door swung open and her father was there to help them all out, bemused to be wearing a fitted tuxedo, a beaming smile on his craggy, weather-beaten face, delighted to be there, as proud as punch of his only child.

As soon as they were all standing, Agon's glorious spring sun shining on them, the girls fussed with her dress, making sure there were no wrinkles around her protruding bump.

Carrie was six months pregnant. It was a year to the day since she and Andreas had exchanged their vows in the Chelsea registry office with two strangers acting as their witnesses.

When they had gone to visit his parents to share their happy news, his mother had promptly burst into tears. Those tears were only pacified when Andreas had promised they would do it all over again, properly. And by properly he meant a full church wedding with his entire family in attendance, everyone congregating to the same hotel afterwards and everyone then meeting the happy couple for breakfast.

As Carrie had taken an instant shine to both of his parents she had been happy to go along with the plans for them but then, as the date neared, found herself excited for hers and Andreas's own sake.

A big white wedding, surrounded by friends and family, the people who loved them, everyone wishing them well…

It had been a strange experience, being embraced into the bosom of the Samaras family, especially as her own was so small. She hadn't properly appreciated what a close-knit family they all were, not until she and Andreas had moved to Agon permanently a few months ago and found their villa under constant siege from aunts, uncles and cousins all inviting themselves round for a holiday. Anyone would think they weren't all scattered on varying Greek islands with their own beautiful beaches a short walk away. Andreas had since bought the neighbouring villa for his family to use so they could have some privacy. Their only real houseguests now were his parents, Violet and Natalia.

Her sister and his niece were tentatively re-kindling their old friendship. Both were doing well. Violet had decided to stay in California permanently. She was still clean. Every day was still a battle but, she had assured Carrie, it was a battle that was getting easier. She *wanted* to stay clean. She wanted to live a long, healthy life. Her words were music to Carrie's ears.

As for Carrie, she'd handed her notice in when they moved to Agon. She had come to love their home there, loved the life, the sunshine, everything about it. Somewhere along the way she had lost her drive for investigative journalism and, anyway, it wasn't as if she could go undercover any more when she was half of a famous couple. Her exclusive feature on Andreas—he had *loved* it—had been a huge hit and the features editor had offered her freelance work, interviewing business leaders and politicians. With Andreas's encouragement, Carrie had been delighted to accept.

The church doors swung open, the organ started to play and, her arm securely in her father's hold, her free hand resting on her kicking baby, she began the slow walk to her husband to repeat the vows they had made in private to the rest of the world.

Andreas stood at the top of the aisle next to his father, who was acting as his best man. The two Samaras men had identical beaming grins.

Her heart skipped to see him.

Her heart *always* skipped to see him.

She had never believed heaven existed.

With Andreas she had found it.

* * * * *

If you enjoyed
A BRIDE AT HIS BIDDING
we're sure you'll love Michelle Smart's
BOUND TO A BILLIONAIRE *trilogy!*

PROTECTING HIS DEFIANT INNOCENT
CLAIMING HIS ONE-NIGHT BABY
BUYING HIS BRIDE OF CONVENIENCE

Available now!

Get 2 Free Books,
Plus 2 Free Gifts—
just for trying the
Reader Service!

HRLP17R3

Get 2 Free Books,
Plus 2 Free Gifts -
just for trying the Reader Service!

Get 2 Free Books,
Plus 2 Free Gifts—
just for trying the Reader Service!